Tales of Illeross: A Mother's Prayer

Ellie Lerum

Red Richard Arts

To all the families wanting desperately to expand, and feeling so alone in your grieving.

You're not alone.

Author's Note

Many readers lift a book and wonder why they should trust the author, regardless of genre. Non-fiction books tend to have a rougher time, given that their authors should be at least reasonably versed on the topic. Fiction tends to be slightly more forgiving, though topics such as miscarriage, infertility, and birth are often shied away from as they are controversial.

Anca's story mirrors many aspects of my own journey to bring my two girls into the world. This said, absolutely none of this book is meant to trivialize experiences the reader may have, nor are these written words meant to minimize the pain that individuals go through while attempting to expand their family. This is simply a fictional account of what I went through; a glimpse into real pain, faith that does tremble, and the raw human emotion that I underwent.

If Anca's story shines a light on your own experiences, please know that you aren't alone. Statistics don't often mean much, but the numbers 1 in 4, or 1 in 8, do; we don't ever realize how big of a statistic those truly are, nor do we fully understand why we may become a part of the statistics themselves.

Miscarriage, infertility, and pregnancy loss are no jokes. As I shared in a different novel, my husband and I lost six pregnancies amid having two children. Recently, I received word from two women who I hold very near to my heart that they, too, lost their pregnancies. The difference between my loss and theirs? They knew I had mourned, and so they had people they could mourn with. I didn't have that blessing.

As you read Anca's story, *A Mother's Prayer*, please know that my heart goes to you if you resonate with any of the happenings in these pages. If you are in the midst of this trying season, or you are waiting, please know that you're not alone. I understand, at least in part, the pain you are going through. I also know that God hears you, and He mourns with you.

If you are in a place in which you need additional help, please reach out to the National Maternal Mental Health Hotline (U.S.).

- U.S. National Maternal Mental Health Hotline: 1-833-852-6262

God bless,
Ellie

Contents

Chapter One

Settling

After what felt like an eternity of pain, there seemed to finally be a breath of fresh air.

Anca slowly turned and took in their new home. She nodded to herself. It was smaller than what her stepchildren—Drop and Shatter—were used to. Still, it was a roof over their heads in a place that wouldn't persecute them. That was the most important part.

"Well?" Her husband, Flick, asked softly from behind her. "What do you think? I know it isn't nearly as nice as what we had in Zanther, but there's a bedchamber for us, and eventually the children can receive one as well. It was all they could do on short notice."

She looked at the man.

He was still bandaged from the beating he had received from his father, and each wound was a reminder of the hatred that Solari worshippers clung to. The nation of Zanther was hostile toward anything that spoke against their gods, especially if it involved the outlawed god HaMelech. Their regime stemmed from the worship of many false gods, and actively speaking against them brought a fate worse than death.

Despite this, his eyes still shone with a light that Anca hadn't seen since the day they were wed.

Married.

Anca's head still swam at the reminder. Their marriage hadn't been too long ago, but it still felt like it had taken an eternity while they were in Zanther. She pushed those thoughts away as Flick wrapped one arm around her waist. "I think this is just what we need," she murmured. "As you said, it isn't what you and the children were used to, but this will do for us. It's just the four of us, as of current."

Flick smiled beside her, and she leaned her head against his chest. That would change, soon enough. They wanted a child together, one to bring their family to completion.

Outside, Anca caught the sounds of Drop and Shatter laughing among other children. She looked over her shoulder, smiling a little to herself. "They've bounced back."

"I'm glad... he was horrible to them," Flick whispered. Anca looked at him and pressed closer. "I still can't believe that he was willing to starve them—"

"He was a man delusional with power and demonic forces, Flick," Anca whispered. "HaMelech willing, one day he might be saved. Until then, all we can do is forgive him for what he did to us, and pray that he sees his sins." Her husband chuckled softly, shaking his head, and Anca sighed. It was a bigger task than she wanted to admit, but she knew their God, HaMelech, could work mighty miracles. Whether that miracle was one that He would perform, though, she didn't know.

What she did know, though, was that this time was miraculous. Their family was free from Fernando Alastar's chains—literal or otherwise. Anca looked at her husband, searching his face. He wouldn't admit the pain his father caused, would he? If it had been any other High Inquisitor who had imprisoned and abused them, the hurt would eventually fade. Coming from Flick's father, though, Anca was sure it would linger for decades at the very least.

Drop and Shatter came thundering in, their clothes coated in dust and grass stains from running with the others. Anca crouched to receive them, holding the two close as she stroked down their black hair. Her stepdaughter, Drop, who was six, beamed at her. After so many months of being ill, before Anca had met their father, it was hard to imagine this same child had been on death's doorstep. Now, her wide eyes were the vision of life. Shatter, smaller than his older sister as he was only five, clung to Anca with one hand. He sucked on his thumb, a habit that Anca knew they'd need to break eventually, before he looked at Flick. "Papa?"

"Come here," Flick chuckled.

He lifted the boy as Anca took Drop's hand, and the small family slowly explored their home.

The floors were still dirt. With fall in full swing, there wasn't enough time to add a cellar or wood planking. Sturdy pine planks made the walls, and the rafters smelled strongly of freshly cut oak. Rolandus, one of Flick's friends, had given them polished box bed, their most precious furniture. The wood shone golden in the light of the gas lamp, a silent reminder of the blessing of the gift.

It was small, but it was home.

A little tap on the ajar door prompted Anca to turn to see that Rolandus was there. His dreadlocked hair had been tied back from his face, and his eyes shone with kindness. Beside him was Marin, the redheaded healer who Anca owed her salvation in HaMelech to. Her friend had her arm linked with Rolandus in a fondness, though guarded, as she held a basket. "Are you free for a moment?"

"Of course, anything for family," Anca said. She passed Drop to Flick, who had begun to play with Shatter on the packed earth floor, and crossed to them. There, she gave Marin a tight hug. "This is perfect, thank you."

"We'll be sure to pass your thanks on to the carpenter who helped," Marin said, squeezing her. "We wanted to make sure that you had food for the evening. I made some bread, and Rolandus brought some cider. Olare would have come with us to check in, but he was called into a meeting."

"How's his arm?" Anca murmured.

Marin's brother, Olare, had lost his arm while escaping Zanther with them. The injuries their group had sustained were limited to him—Rolandus and Flick had managed to remain unscathed in any of the fights. Olare himself was fortunate enough to be fit for a prosthetic, but that didn't mean that his spirits were still high.

"He'll be alright once he comes to terms with it," Rolandus said quietly. "I think his biggest disappointment is losing the use of his longsword." He smiled slightly at Marin, who had looked down. Anca's heart ached for her friend. There were a lot of changes that came from their escape, especially in knowing that their wounds would take time to heal.

She took Marin's hand and held it. "Would you like to eat with us? I don't have too terribly much, but we can check the orchards for some apples... and I'm sure the community garden has some produce we can use."

"I would like to, yes," Marin said. She followed Anca inside and placed the basket down. Then, she looked at Rolandus. "Did you want to stay with Flick and the children?"

The man looked up from where he was, already holding Shatter in his arms. He gave a sheepish grin. "I think so."

Anca laughed, kissed Flick lightly as she threw her shawl over her shoulders, and followed Marin out.

Her husband seemed at peace with the children, and that brought her joy. Still, there was the desire to have more while they had all they needed. Anca didn't like clinging to those thoughts, but she found herself dwelling on the idea of carrying her own child. Flick was already an excellent father; would she be a good mother? Drop and Shatter seemed easy enough to tend to, especially being four and three.

Marin cleared her throat, pulling Anca from her thoughts. "So... how long do you think it'll be before Flick decides to lead a patrol into Zanther?"

A shiver flooded through Anca, and she swallowed. "I'm not ready for him to go back, regardless of his purpose. His father tried to kill him; if he's found out, they won't merely torture him." Still, she knew that Flick's mission in Zanther could save thousands of lives that would otherwise be executed. Her heart clenched, and she looked down, sucking in a breath. Thousands of Kingsmen, like her friend Catherine, or her friend's young daughter, Annabel, were burned at the stake for heresy.

Anger burned in Anca for a brief moment before she exhaled.

Justice was for HaMelech to deliver, not her. For all she knew, those who had killed the Kingsmen would be saved; only HaMelech could answer that question.

"Anca?"

Marin put her hand on Anca's arm, and she glanced at her friend. Then, she whispered, "I don't want him to return, Marin. I don't want to lose my husband again, not after only getting him back recently."

"Oh, Anca." The redhead pulled Anca into an embrace, and Anca closed her eyes. She sniffled, doing her best to keep from crying, as Marin whispered, "HaMelech will protect him. He always has, with each patrol that goes out. His ways are so much higher than our own."

"I know... I know..." Anca pulled away and wiped her eyes, then looked at the sky. "It'll be alright. I... I want there to be a future for our family. For Drop, and Shatter, and any children we have together."

Her friend smiled knowingly at her before the two began to walk again. They were silent as they entered the community garden to collect a cabbage and carrots, and then wandered to the butcher. A small package of pork wasn't too expensive, but Anca felt guilty spending some of their meager funds to pay for it. She could cook some tonight, salt the rest, and keep it for bacon. It wouldn't go to waste, and they'd be able to use it again. Then, the two made their way towards the small home that Flick and the children remained in.

Before they reached it, Anca looked at Marin. "You wanted to know what the future might hold for Flick and I. What about you and Rolandus? Are you going to go through with your engagement, now that we're here?"

A little hum answered her, and Marin shook her head. Anca frowned as the redhead murmured, "HaMelech has a new season for us both. We made a promise to obey HaMelech before we agreed to wed, and we have yet to be released from our calls to enter marriage. Our engagement is still there, but it will not come to fruition for a time."

"Isn't that hard, the wait?"

"It is... but that will make the time so much sweeter," Marin said. She smiled at Anca and nudged her. "You and Flick have a season you will be waiting for, I have no doubt. I can see how you'd like to be a mother to a child you've carried."

Anca looked down, and she smiled. "I'm excited for that season. I love Drop and Shatter, they are everything... but a little sibling for them would be wonderful. I know Flick would like to have another one, too."

The two bumped each other with a small laugh, and Marin beamed. "I'll be here for you the entire time. Praying, listening, and doing whatever I can. You're my sister."

Her soft words made Anca smile, though she knew it didn't reach her eyes. She did have a blood sister, Adriata, but after renouncing the supposed god Solaris in front of her, Anca doubted that the word 'sister' was accurate. Marin seemed to sense this as she gently embraced her, and Anca pressed her face into the other woman's neck. Marin sighed and squeezed her. "There's no point in obsessing over the past," she whispered. "HaMelech will move as He will, and bring paths together as needed. He will make all things good."

"I know."

They returned to the humble cottage to find that Flick and Rolandus had exhausted themselves with Drop and Shatter. While still awake, the two men were lying on the dirt floor while the children played with their hair. When Anca and Marin entered, the little ones looked up and ran to them. Anca caught them both and held them, closing her eyes as she savored their hugs. Shatter nuzzled in while Drop, ever as sweet, kissed her cheek.

This was home.

The remainder of the evening was spent cooking some of the pork and vegetables, and laying the remainder of the pork with salt to preserve it. Flick did what he could to shuffle furniture around their humble home; a rickety table and four spindly chairs had been put in the middle of the room. Anca smiled back at him, receiving a grin in return, and then returned to her tasks. Eventually, they laid Drop and Shatter in the bedbox and closed the door. Marin and Rolandus left well before bedtime, leaving the two to sink onto an understuffed sofa together. Anca leaned against her husband, and he ran a hand through her hair as he sighed and closed his eyes.

"We made it," Anca whispered. "We have so little, outside of our health, but it's there."

Flick chuckled quietly. "From what I've heard from others, that's more than enough."

Anca nodded against him, turned to rest against his side, and closed her own eyes. "We'll make it a home. We've got the children, and we have each other; we will be alright."

Again, Flick nodded, and they rested quietly. Eventually, Anca pulled away to fetch the knitting she'd been working on. Flick began to clean his wooden staff, and the two glanced at one another with a little smile before going back to their tasks.

Morning came quickly, and Anca found herself between Flick and Drop, both of whom were snoring.

They would need to get a second box bed before long.

Anca slipped from the bed to wash her face and get ready for the day. Her apron went on easily and she made porridge, pausing to finish the pork from the night before. As her family slept, she slipped outside beneath the apple tree beside their home and knelt to pray.

It felt better to be outside for this prayer, even if there was a Temple not far from their home. It reminded Anca of first encountering and accepting HaMelech, surrounded by His creation.

"HaMelech, my king," she whispered. The wind rustled the leaves above her, and she smiled slightly to herself.

His presence was everywhere.

Anca sighed and shifted to get comfortable again. "Father, thank you for our home, the garden that we will tend to, and the children that we are raising. Thank you for the harvest that the town has received and the apples we will soon pick. You are a good father and a provider. Steady my hands as I work today, and help me to support Flick as his bride. Our life is finally becoming some semblance of normal, and..." she paused, her voice catching. Was she scared of this? She really shouldn't be scared; she knew she was safe with Flick, especially after everything that had happened. Perhaps she was nervous about disappointing him? No, she shouldn't be worried about that, either. She knew that his approval, while nice, didn't at all compare to HaMelech's approval. Anca frowned to herself and sighed. "I don't know what to do," she finally murmured. "I think I'm afraid of doing everything wrong. I don't want to disappoint him, I don't want to fail the children... HaMelech, I'm so afraid that I have stepped into something I'm wholly unprepared for."

The wind rustled the leaves again, kicking a few stray pieces that had decided to fall early into Anca's face. She kept her eyes closed even during the intrusion before she hung her head. "You will guide me, You will keep me safe... Please, take these feelings and hold them. Help me to face them and remind me of Your truth as we move into this new life. Amen."

She stood, brushed her hands off, and looked at the sky. It was a busy day to begin, and there were things that had yet to even be thought about since they escaped from Zanther.

When Anca returned to the home, she carefully woke the children to get them dressed and tidy the floor. A pot of water was on the fire for Flick's bath, and she smiled to herself as she heard him roll over in their bed with a groan. This was perhaps the best sleep they'd had in a while, too.

Soon enough, the day had begun, and they were all awake. Anca sent Drop and Shatter from the house to play as soon as she heard the giggles of children outside their door. With the kids gone, she began to scrub the porridge pot out, elbow deep in lye. Halfway through the endeavor, Flick gave her a kiss. "I need to go help Rolandus this morning with training the young ones."

"Are you training them to go to Zanther?" Anca asked, looking up at him. Was he going to leave sooner than she had assumed? She wasn't entirely sure when he'd leave, but the idea of having him return to Zanther so soon frightened her.

Flick paused, his eyebrows knit together, before they relaxed. "Soon enough," he murmured. "These pupils are currently too young to make the trek, not without their parents. I will be aiding him in two months' time, though, in preparing a patrol. Olare also asked me to consider serving in Bleak Hollow for a term." He turned away to pull his boots on, and Anca began to wring the kitchen towel in her hands. "It'll be alright, Anca. HaMelech will prepare us."

"I don't want to lose you again, not after only recently returning to your side," Anca murmured. The fear gnawed at her again, making her swallow. "Flick, I don't want you to return to Zanther if you can avoid it. Bleak Hollow... while it isn't ideal, I'd rather face chittering demons a thousand times over than to risk you encountering that man..."

"Anca, I'll be okay," Flick soothed. He finished dressing and kissed the top of her head. "It'll be alright, I swear. HaMelech is in control, is he not?"

The smaller blonde looked up at him, searching his dark eyes, before she sighed and nodded. "You're right, and I know that this fear isn't of Him. I was praying earlier this morning and... the worries are there. I need Him to take them—"

"Then let's give them to Him, Anca," Flick interrupted softly. He gathered her hands into his own, the comfort making Anca sigh and bow her head, and then he murmured, "HaMelech, we're afraid. You didn't make us to be creatures of fear, and so we give them to You. Our worries about the future, the 'what-ifs', the maybes, are for You to take. Help us to keep them at your feet." He paused for a moment, squeezed Anca's hands, and murmured, "I pray protection over this household, Lord. Spread Your wings over our children so they may experience Your world in safety. Continue to guide Anca as she raises them in the home." One of his hands released Anca's, and she shifted, finding that he had placed it on her belly. "Grant us peace as we wait to welcome another child to this family. Guard Anca as we make these choices, keep her safe and help her thrive as we move towards the life you've called us towards." Anca placed her hand on his own as Flick ran a thumb back and forth under hers. It was a gentle gesture, and Anca knew that, with even that prayer, Flick was hoping to father a child with her. There was no doubt that he wanted to complete their family, and Anca nearly let an invitation slip from her lips. He needed to work, though, and as he murmured a quiet 'amen', she whispered her agreement and embraced him.

Her husband held her close, and Anca pressed her face to his chest until he released her. "I'll be home within a handful of hours," he said. "Once I'm back, I was hoping to get a garden set up for you. It's too late in the season to plant, but at the very least we can decide where you'd like it and get a fence made."

"Alright," Anca said.

She watched him leave, gave a sigh, and closed her eyes. They both knew he'd go back, she'd be alright.

The rest of the day moved smoothly. Drop and Shatter played beside Anca as she scrubbed their laundry. The creek wound on one side of the town, providing cool air amid the warm autumn day. As Anca worked, little feet sent water flying about as the children splashed. A handful of other mothers and their children were there, too, chatting as lye burned their hands. After washing was hung on bushes outside of their home, Anca sent the two out with a small lunch and five smooth pebbles to play with. With them entertained, Anca started a loaf of bread and began to reheat the soup from the night prior. By the time Flick came down the path, she had settled on a chair outside to embroider and watch the children draw in the dirt. Drop and Shatter flew to him, and Anca followed behind. He embraced them each, kissed Anca, and they finished the evening together.

After the children had been put to bed, Flick sat beside Anca on the sofa once more. "My love?"

"Yes?"

"Earlier, I prayed about a season of waiting." Flick tilted his head toward her, and Anca blushed slightly as she worked. "When do you want to try expanding our family?"

When did she? Was now the right time? Did HaMelech want them to wait? She didn't want to disobey His will, but He did ask His creations to multiply and subdue the earth. It was a matter of timing at this point. Anca shifted, then looked at Flick. His face was the vision of gentleness, and her eyes softened as he rested a hand on her leg. "I want nothing more than to have a child with you," she murmured, "but I don't know if now is the correct time. HaMelech will bless us in His timing, though, and I trust that it will happen."

"Then we will get the children a box bed, and we can attempt to bring another life into this family," Flick decided.

The words made Anca's heart flutter, and she nodded. "Can we do that tomorrow? Start the process so they may have their space before the snow falls?"

"Of course."

Anca lay awake after they retired for the night, listening to Flick's soft snoring beside her. They were going to have a baby. Drop and Shatter would have a younger brother or sister. They would be so close in age, too, which would be wonderful! With those thoughts, Anca drifted into a peaceful sleep.

Chapter Two

Six Months

It had been six months since Anca and Flick had first moved into their home. Gone were the falling leaves and, instead, were the beautiful flowers of the apple trees and plants that surrounded their plot of land. Drop and Shatter each celebrated a birthday in that span of time, turning seven and six respectively. Anca remained home with the children, though her heart ached with each passing day.

They had yet to conceive.

She stared anxiously at the small pile of barley Marin had supplied her to test for pregnancy, the same pile she had used two days ago. There were no sprouts, just as before. Flick lightly knocked on the door. "Anca?"

She was silent as she brushed the barley, now dry, into a small sack she had been using for rubbish. Then, after running her hands under a stream of water to clean them, she quietly moved to the door. She did her best to give Flick a smile, but the moment she attempted, she knew it wasn't enough. Her husband pulled her into his arms and pressed his face into her hair. "Still nothing?"

"Nothing," she whispered.

Hot tears streaked down her face at the words, and she squeezed her eyes closed to keep from crying anymore. She was tired of the tears, of the heartbreak. It was hard to keep hope after six months, but she knew it was also foolish to despair over it. Others tried for longer, after all, and she was fortunate enough to know that HaMelech would provide should it be in His will. Flick rubbed her back as she stood there, and he kissed her head several times before he breathed, "We can try again later, my love."

"We can," she whispered back, "though I know you are to serve in Bleak Hollow soon. Would it be wise to potentially conceive when you are going to the most dangerous place in Dusnar?"

Flick hummed at her before he sighed. "That's true." He pulled away to wipe at her eyes. "Why don't we go sit in the shade of the tree outside and watch Drop and Shatter? They're playing with frogs they found in the creek, and it's been rather sweet to watch."

"We can do that," Anca whispered.

It had been hard to watch the children enjoy themselves. Anca loved them dearly, but the sight of their relationship with Flick made it ever harder for her to deal with her inability to have children at this time. It was only six months, though, and that could have been lingering stress from Zanther. At least, that's what Marin had said the last time she had visited. Marin knew better than Anca, given her training. Perhaps it was HaMelech's grace in having them wait. If Flick did go to Bleak Hollow, and she was pregnant, she'd have to undergo that entire endeavor while he was gone. Even with his service being a month in that horrid place, surrounded by demons, it was still a month that Anca would worry sick about his return.

She sighed and sat down beneath the tree, leaning against Flick. Drop and Shatter did indeed have frogs, and as Shatter caught one with a triumphant cry, she couldn't help but smile at her son. They were so innocent, not knowing the pain that she and Flick were undergoing.

Anca prayed that the events of Zanther, weeks of being starved and beaten, would be nothing more than a distant, hazy memory for them, too. HaMelech was good, and He knew what to do to best help them. Drop raced to Anca, holding a frog in her hands. "Mamma! Mamma, look!"

The frog let out a defiant squeal, making Drop drop it with a squeak of her own, and it landed solidly in Anca's lap. The sudden intruder made Anca jump, very nearly crushing the amphibian, as Drop began to scream. Flick swiftly scooped the frog from Anca's apron, holding it in two hands as it gave another defiant sound, before he grimaced. "It peed on me."

"It peed?" Shatter questioned, carrying his frog to them.

Anca looked down at her lap, where little splotches of liquid from the frog fell onto her apron. "And, with that, I do believe we may need to be done with the frogs."

***

Life remained chaotic in that way as the season began to change once more. As the first leaves began to fall, Anca watched Flick hoist his pack onto a war ram. Drop and Shatter clung to her skirts as they stood beside her, their eyes wide. It was the first time Flick had left since they arrived in Apple Ridge, and a month-long term in Bleak Hollow would be wearing on him. Anca was grateful that it was only a month, especially given the monsters that lurked where he would serve. Now, as she watched her husband, she shifted. "Are you certain that your mantle will be enough to keep Solari guard from recognizing you? I can only imagine how big the bounty on your head is now," she said softly.

Flick smiled, a knowing look in his eye. "I'll be alright. I didn't use my mantle often in Zanther, and when I did, no one knew it was me." He smoothed the feathers over his shoulders down, quiet for a moment. "They won't be able to recognize me if I'm careful... and if they do, my prayer is that HaMelech will confuse them long enough for me to make an escape."

He was fortunate to be a cote, Anca decided. If he wasn't, there'd be no way to shift his appearance into the raven-person he could be. It was an additional protection for their family, one that HaMelech had so carefully orchestrated. Anca nodded slightly and gently pulled away from the children to kiss Flick. He held her tightly, pressing his forehead to her own as the kiss ended, and sighed. "I'll be back before you know it."

Anca nodded as Drop and Shatter joined them, one of her hands falling to stroke their dark hair down as Flick held her. Finally, the man murmured, "Father, HaMelech, King of Kings, we stand before You humbly. We love You, we are so grateful to You for the blessings You've given us. Thank you for the protection that You will provide as I serve in Bleak Hollow with others from this town, and thank you for the opportunities we have to share Your love with those who don't know You.

"Watch over this family as we are separated for a time, especially Drop and Shatter. Keep them from trouble, help them to obey, and bring them closer to You. Protect Anca, and help her to cherish this time away from me as a moment of worship to You. We will see each other again soon, and until then, I pray nothing but blessings and fruitfulness over our family. Amen."

He mounted his war ram, rode it to join the others in the patrol leaving, and waved back to the family. Anca held the children close as they waved, her heart aching for her husband. As they watched, she whispered, "HaMelech, protect my husband. Bring him home safely to me."

***

Anca's monthly course was late, and when it arrived, it was far heavier than she'd ever experienced. As she laid in her bed, unable to move as her back spasmed and cramped, a little knock rang on the door. Drop and Shatter looked up from their corn husk dolls. "Mamma?"

"I'll get it, my love," Anca murmured. She peeled herself from the comfort of her bed and slowly moved to the door. One hand clutched her shawl as she opened the heavy barrier, blinking as she saw Marin on the other side. "I didn't expect to see you."

"I received mail from Olare in Bleak Hollow," Marin replied. She smiled before it faded. "You look miserable... here, take a seat."

"Thank you," Anca said. She sank into a chair and looked at the children. "Why don't you two go outside, hm? Stay beside the garden; I don't want you to wander too far today." The children nodded as they hurried away, each giving Anca a tight hug, and then slipped from the house. Once they were out, Anca looked at Marin. "I'm sorry, it's been an incredibly long week. I feel like this is the worst monthly course since before I was wed."

Marin frowned slightly, and then, gently, asked, "Was it on time?"

Anca paused, then shook her head. Her friend didn't need to say a word as realization crept over Anca and she slowly covered her mouth. Before she could stop them, hot and angry tears streaked down Anca's face. Not even choking them back helped, and she began to sob beside Marin.

She was losing a pregnancy.

Outside, she could hear the echoes of laughter coming from Drop and Shatter. They didn't know what was happening inside, nor would they; this wasn't their burden to bear, no matter how lonely Anca felt in this moment. Marin enveloped her in a tight hug, making Anca cling to her. "Oh, Anca... I'm so, so sorry."

Anca merely shook her head. She wanted desperately to question HaMelech, to ask Him why this was happening after so many months of waiting. She hadn't even known of this life that was growing within her, and then it was being stripped away from her. Flick wasn't here, he didn't know. Was she going to tell him? Did she want to spare him of the pain, or should she bring him into the grief? It had been his child, too; keeping it from him would bring nothing but distrust and pain, more than she was willing to deal with herself. Marin continued to hold her, rubbing her back, and eventually Anca whispered, "It is good news from Bleak Hollow, isn't it? Please, say that it's good news."

Her friend nodded slightly. "They're returning home in the next week."

One week. It would be another week before Flick was home, before Anca could sob into his chest. One week.

She pulled away, slowly, and wiped her face. "Alright... alright, one week before they're back."

"Anca—"

"I... I think I need to be alone, Marin," Anca whispered. She shifted, wiped her eyes, and swallowed. "I appreciate you bringing me the news from Bleak Hollow and..."

"And you need to grieve," Marin murmured back. She nodded slightly, pressed Anca's hand, and whispered, "I'm here for you as you mourn. When you're ready, I'll be here to listen."

"Thank you," Anca breathed. She shut her eyes, her voice catching, and she took a breath. "I... I want to pray with you before you go, though. It's about the only thing I can cling to with this, and I want to pray with you."

Marin shifted closer, not saying a word as she got comfortable. Then, as she held Anca, she finally spoke. "HaMelech... grief is horrid. It wasn't meant to be a part of this world, and you never wanted us to experience it. Anca is in the depths of mourning; mourning for a child, mourning for a desire. Please, envelop her with your peace and your wisdom. Hold her tightly, heal her heart and her body, and help each of us to lean into you even further." Anca nodded slightly, realizing that she was shaking as Marin held her. The sounds of footsteps on the packed dirt floor made her slowly lift her head, finding that Drop and Shatter had come in to look at them with wide eyes.

She pulled away from Marin and held her arms out. "I'm alright, it's okay."

"Why are you crying?" Drop asked, holding tightly to her. Shatter didn't speak as he cuddled into her side, though his eyes were huge as he stared at Anca.

The woman forced a smile on her face and then shook her head. They didn't need to know what could have been. It wasn't theirs to know, nor was it a burden that she wished them to share. Instead, Anca murmured, "I'm simply having a hard day, my loves. But, Marin brought good news! Papa will be home soon, as will Uncle Rolandus and Uncle Olare!"

Drop and Shatter nearly vibrated with excitement, a momentary reprieve from Anca's heartbreak. She hugged them tightly, closed her eyes, and sighed.

When Flick did return, after he embraced Drop and Shatter, she fell into his arms and clung tightly to him. She could feel a handful of bandages beneath his tunic, prompting her to close her eyes tightly, and she simply held onto him as he wrapped his arms around her. Finally, he pulled away with a smile. Then, as he searched her face, his smile faded. "What happened?"

"I... not in front of Drop and Shatter, please," Anca murmured. He frowned but nodded, stroking her cheek as a rogue tear streaked down it.

That night, he and Anca played a simple stacking game with Drop and Shatter before the children climbed into their bed and shut the little door on the bedbox. Anca sat silently as Flick sat beside her. Before he could question her, though, she murmured, "How bad was Bleak Hollow?"

"It wasn't bad; we did have a couple of moments where the chitters were heavy, but we lost no pilgrims, nor did we lose any of our ranks. Rolandus recounted a rather nasty chitter he had dealt with before, but it still hadn't reformed after Olare killed it," Flick said. He rubbed his shoulder where the bandages were, grimacing. "I did have an issue with a Solari guard, may HaMelech forgive him, but it wasn't due to who I was. They decided that they were threatened by our patrol when we refused to take any additional travelers due to lack of guards."

Anca frowned. If fights were breaking out in Dusnar, that was a problem; a treaty was in place to protect Kingsmen and Solari alike, especially as tensions grew high again. A war would do nothing but destroy the nation, and then Yegreydal would move in with the Inquisitors from Zanther. She swallowed, offered a quick prayer to HaMelech, and then looked at Flick. "I'm so incredibly glad you're safely home."

"As am I... though... I can tell that something's wrong. The whole house feels heavy, and I can see something's weighing on you." Flick took Anca's hand, holding it. She looked down and he tilted her chin back up. "Anca, what happened?"

It took a moment for Anca to gather her courage. She hated her hands shaking as they were, even when Flick held them. She felt lightheaded, struggling to stay conscious, and she swallowed past the lump in her throat before she whispered, "I was pregnant, and I lost the pregnancy."

Her words hung in the air. She didn't dare look up at Flick as he sat in silence, not wanting to watch the disappointment and grief flood his face. As his hand tightened on hers, she knew that it was hitting him. Finally, he pulled her into a tight hug. Anca felt tears sting her eyes again as his shoulders shook, prompting her to cling to Flick once more as they began to cry. Finally, amid their sobs, Flick breathed, "I'm so sorry I wasn't here for you."

Neither of them spoke as they held onto one another, and finally Flick pulled away to wipe Anca's cheeks and kiss her head. He didn't say a word again, and neither did Anca. She appreciated his silence; it was quieting the voices in her own mind, the ones demanding that she say that it was her fault, that she had done this to herself. He was a grounding force, radiating love and gentleness even in the pain that they felt. As he kissed her forehead again, Anca sniffled and looked down. "I need you to tell me that I shouldn't feel guilty, please."

"Why should you feel guilty?" Flick stroked her cheeks again. "Anca, you did nothing to be at fault for a miscarriage. I don't know why it happened, but I know you cannot blame yourself. There is no guilt to be had."

"We wanted a baby, and I lost one."

"And we will recover; HaMelech is still faithful, you are loved deeply by Him and I. We haven't been forgotten in our grief, we won't be abandoned in our mourning."

Anca slowly nodded, inhaling, and Flick pet her hair. "You are a wonderful mother, Anca. HaMelech will bless us with a child to hold in time. For now, we mourn, we pray, and we remember."

"You're right."

They bowed their heads together and prayed, and all the while Anca struggled to focus. Her mind was filled with all of the lies, all of the whispers, and all of the what-ifs. Maybe, just maybe, she could have carried that baby longer if she had done something different. Then, in the midst of the whispers, a feeling of peace washed over her, and she closed her eyes. HaMelech was there, and this would be okay eventually.

***

Several months passed and, with them, Anca and Flick continued to mourn. Their joy in Drop and Shatter remained, but it was still painful as Anca experienced two more miscarriages, and then bleeding for two months. She didn't wish to smile, she didn't wish to leave the home. Some of the women had begun murmuring about her while doing washing, and so she withdrew from even that task. Flick did what he could to reassure her and ease the pain, but Anca often shook her head and turned away. She wished nothing more than to spare him from the grief that continued to come.

Eventually, Anca sank to her knees in the Temple of HaMelech. She hadn't been able to sleep; it'd been several months since she had last properly rested. Marin had recommended some herbs to use before resting, the same ones she had survivors of chittering madness take, but Anca didn't want to. She honestly wasn't sure what she wanted; she knew she hurt, she knew she was grieving, and she knew that she desperately wanted to feel like it would be okay again. And, so, she knelt before the altar in the Temple and wept.

They were hot, bitter tears. Her cries echoed through the stone building, and she eventually threw her head back. "Why, HaMelech?

"Three miscarriages, two months of bleeding, so many more months of not conceiving! Why? HaMelech, it *hurts*! It hurts to be in this state, it hurts to see the sadness on Flick's face, it hurts trying to love Drop and Shatter when I cannot even love myself!" Anca clung to her skirt, her shawl providing little comfort against the cool air coming from the partially open windows. Her fingers were aching as she held onto any semblance of grounding that she could, and she sucked in a breath. "Why is this happening? Why is the world so broken that You are allowing this? What lesson must I learn, what area is it that I must grow in?"

She hung her head, sobbing once more. The Holy Texts promised that HaMelech would understand even the groans that she gave, when words didn't function, and she finally sighed. "Please, HaMelech, I can't do this. I can't bear the pain any longer than I must, and it frightens me."

HaMelech was listening, right? Anca sniffled and curled into a ball before the altar. He was listening, He saw her pain, and He promised to wipe every tear from her face. Why, then, did she feel so alone? It was the world, the Black Dragon, whispering that He wasn't good. They were lies, lies that He didn't care and that she had been abandoned. "HaMelech, You promise to gather every tear I weep. You promised so many women in the Holy Texts that they would receive a child, and You do not lie.

"Please, my God, please promise me the same. Bless me with a child I may raise beside their siblings, a child that we can teach Your law alongside Drop and Shatter. I so desperately want to give them a sibling to love and protect especially as I see the longing in their eyes and the jealousy that is there when other children speak of their younger family members. HaMelech, bless my womb, make me fruitful. Bring me closer to you through the miracle of childbirth, let me..." she trailed off, sighed, and shook her head.

She was demanding, not asking. It was a poor position to place her heart, especially when she had so many blessings that she was overlooking. Finally, after several moments, she breathed, "Forgive me for my hubris. Forgive me of my attitude, and my shortsightedness. HaMelech, I am in pain, and I am in mourning... it isn't an excuse, as I know that You are well aware of where my heart is. So, Father, I ask for Your blessing on the family You have given me. Thank you for Shatter and Drop. They are growing so quickly and into such strong children.

I pray that they will always know Your voice and will desire to follow You as they continue to grow.

"Thank you for Flick, his desire to protect our family while serving You and his desire to show who You are to others. Thank you for the home we have over our heads, the love You provide, and the comfort You have given me in this season. I love You, and I trust You, regardless of the season that You have me growing through.

"Father, if it is in Your will... please, bless us with a third child. Let us rejoice rather than mourn, and bring us all closer to one another... Amen."

Chapter Three

A Year and a Half

Anca did her best to keep her chin up over the next year. Drop and Shatter grew older, her marriage with Flick grew sweeter, but it still felt like their family was missing someone. Now that Drop and Shatter were both old enough to attend school, she spent her days working in the infirmary. Unlike before she was married, she was strictly doing administration work.

It had been eighteen months since they first began trying for a baby. A year and a half. More miscarriages, more negative pregnancy tests, and more tears.

She was doing her best, now, to forget that she and Flick wanted to have a child. Grief moved into a nearly consuming numbness, and so Anca did what she could to focus entirely on her family rather than her desires.

"There we go, Drop," she murmured, helping her stepdaughter back up with a bread paddle. "Easy does it; it gets heavy quickly, and we mustn't drop it."

"Yes, Mamma," Drop said back. The little girl looked at Anca, who gave her a gentle smile.

Drop looked less like Flick and more like her biological mother, but Anca could still see the mischievous quirk of her nose and shine in her eyes that came from her father. Shatter looked more like Flick than not, though he, too, possessed cheekbones that didn't belong to anyone else in their family. It was a strange thought, one that Anca didn't like to dwell on, that these two children knew only her as their mother. It should have brought her comfort, too, rather than the heavy heart that often came with the revelation. A couple of women had commented about it while Anca was doing the washing; she was lucky. She already had two children. HaMelech had blessed her already.

Those words, and the others that whispered through the air, were the only things that really broke the numbness. When they did, they stung worse than a humming badger bite.

She knew full well that gossip had spread like wildfire through the town. Why wouldn't it? As far as Anca knew, she was one of the handful of women who hadn't conceived a child of her own. Certainly, she was the youngest married woman who had yet to bear a child for her husband. It was a bitter reminder as the older women asked when she would secure Flick's lineage.

Fortunately for her, Flick shut those conversations down as soon as he heard them. The man had no tolerance for those statements, snapping finally one day as the women twittered after a church service. Anca quietly drank her cider, watching as Shatter and Drop climbed a nearby tree.

"She's barren, haven't you heard?" came a whisper on the wind. "She has yet to conceive."

"No, I heard she had conceived, but the poor thing simply can't keep them," another said. "I can only imagine how her husband feels."

Anca tightened her grip on her glass, setting her jaw as she stared at the amber liquid. Of course, it would start now. The Holy Texts said that man was blessed when he had a quiver full of children. What did that make Flick, marrying a woman who couldn't bless him with more? The Texts meant it as a comment of HaMelech's goodness, that children were a special blessing from Him. It was never meant to be a statement forcing families into having children, much less to lessen those who couldn't carry.

A couple of laughs echoed, and yet another voice joined. "Do you think Mr. Alastar will walk from her? He seems like a pious man, but not having a child may do enough to serve for a divorce."

Flick stiffened beside Anca, and she glanced at him. He had gritted his teeth, too, and balled his hand into a fist. Anca wrapped her arm with his. "Flick—"

"I will not have them speaking of you this way," he said softly. His eyes held a stern glint, one that Anca typically only saw when the children were disobeying. Then, kissing her forehead, Flick pulled away and strode to the gossiping women.

His voice was strong enough that Anca could hear it from where she stood, though he wasn't attempting to cast all gazes on them. Anca swallowed as she watched him, her cup shaking in her hands.

"Ladies, I will only say this once, especially in that my wife is so incredibly longsuffering with your comments that she has yet to stop your gossiping." Flick put his hands behind his back, his face set in a firm line. "You are to keep her name out of your mouth, as our family is not the source of spectacle. As for whomever it was who thought it wise to question my devotion to her, I pray that HaMelech opens your eyes to your judgmental mindset and keeps you from straying further. I will never, nor have I ever, considered divorce for any reason. If you desire to continue gossiping, then I ask that you refrain from doing it where we can hear and where others will join you." The women he stood before went pale as Flick continued. "Should this matter need to be discussed again, I shall bring another individual into the conversation to call you to account. If even that does not work, I will be bringing this to the church elders. Is that understood?"

Mute nods answered him, and Flick dipped his head. Then, he turned and made his way to Anca. She looked up at him, offered a soft smile, and murmured, "Thank you."

"I will do it as often as I must, though I hope this is the last time," Flick replied. He shook his head, scanning the gathering quietly. Anca could see that he was looking for Drop and Shatter, prompting her to nudge him. He followed her gaze, nodded as he saw the children in the tree, and then looked at Anca. His shoulders relaxed upon finding them. "I hope you know I meant every word I said to them," he said. "I'm not planning on leaving for any reason."

"I believe I know that," Anca said quietly. She shifted and sighed. "It... isn't easy hearing those ideas, though."

"I'm sure it isn't," Flick murmured back. He wrapped an arm around her, and she leaned against his side. Then, he said, "Rolandus and Olare wanted to come to our home, but I had told them that it was up to you. Are you feeling up for visitors at all, or would you rather not?"

Anca sighed at the question. Over the last few weeks, she had wanted to withdraw. She felt bad saying no to company, but she really didn't want to face pity further. Her feelings aside, though, the children missed their adopted uncles, and she did as well. Finally, she nodded. "They may come over. I planned on making some stew this evening, and Drop wanted to help make bread again. She's gotten very good at working with the dough, and I'm incredibly proud of her for all of the help she's given in tending to the garden outside of school. Shatter is making excellent headway on reading, too, and he tried to read a passage of the Holy Texts to me earlier today." She looked up at Flick as he smiled. "They're good children, Flick."

"I know they are, and they have an amazing mother," Flick said softly. He kissed the top of her head, quiet for a moment. "I pray to

HaMelech every night that His will be done, but I'm not sure what even that is. I wish I could do something more to protect you from all the whispers, and the guilt and shame that keep eating at you."

"I don't want to talk about that here." Anca looked away from him and shifted slightly from his side. "Not where others are, please. I don't want anyone to overhear you."

It was shame. Shame was whispering that she had to remain quiet, that they couldn't speak of their troubles in public, and that, if she did, she would be seen as even less than she already was. Anca sighed, closed her eyes, and then inhaled deeply. They had to talk about it. Every time Flick brought it up, she did her best to avoid the topic. She did the same thing to Marin, too, when it came to certain duties, as well as the church. Anca ran a hand through her messy hair and sighed. Perhaps it was time to try and return to things she'd done before?

"Drop, Shatter, time to go!" Flick called.

The children, from the tree, lifted their heads. Drop started down first while Shatter, after a moment, followed her. It was just before he put his foot onto the final branch that he slipped and, with a cry, tumbled to the ground.

There was a resounding gasp from the collected adults, a scream from Drop, and sobs from Shatter all in a handful of moments. Anca and Flick rushed to the tree. "Shatter? Shatter, are you alright?"

"Move out of the way!" Flick scolded as they reached the tree and the small group of children surrounding Shatter. "Let him breathe!"

Anca fell to her knees beside the boy. He was still screaming, his face beet red as he cried, and he was clinging to one of his arms. "Shatter, Shatter, look at me. I need you to breathe, take a deep breath." She pulled him close and tried to inspect his arm. The boy held tighter to himself as Flick settled next to them.

"Hand him to me, I'll hold him so you can look at his arm."

Shatter's screams continued, and soon Marin was with them. "I can't get a good enough look, but I'm almost positive it's broken," Anca said, frowning.

Eyes were beginning to burn in the back of her skull, and Anca could only imagine what people were saying. She hadn't kept their son safe; she should have been watching him closer to be certain that he didn't fall. Why would HaMelech bless them with a child if they couldn't tend to the children they already had?

Anca gritted her teeth at the imagined arguments. HaMelech blesses as He will, and it wasn't contingent on one of the errors she made.

Again, Anca caught herself. She was clinging to reasoning, trying to argue with the lies that she was thinking of. It was her own strength, not that of HaMelech.

Instead of focusing on it any further, she stroked some of Shatter's hair from his face. He continued to sniffle, crying out each time Marin moved his arm. Once he took a breath and calmed down, Anca caught sight of his wrist; the bones were at odd angles and his hand was completely limp. Flick continued to hold their son before he looked at Anca. "I can take him to the Temple for healing if you're alright to take Drop home."

"Are you certain?" Anca glanced at her stepdaughter, who was continuing to stare at her brother with wide eyes. "I can take him if you'd rather."

Marin cleared her throat. "Anca, the pediatric unit is past the maternity ward." She met Anca's gaze, her eyes soft as she murmured, "It may be hard for you to go down that hallway and remain there for long."

Some of Anca's blood boiled, but she sighed and nodded. Marin was looking out for her, wanting desperately to keep her safe and help her to heal from her heartbreak. Flick, though he was also grieving a future that could have been, would likely be able to better handle it all. Besides, Drop would do better being distracted at home with Anca than her father. Flick didn't have much that she could help him with and Anca could at least have her help with dinner.

The woman took Drop's hand as Flick stood with Shatter. No words were exchanged as he and Marin hurried in one direction, and Anca led Drop towards their home.

"Mamma?"

"Yes, my love?"

"Will Shatter be okay?"

"Of course, Drop," Anca said. She smiled gently at the girl, squeezed her hand, and nodded. "Marin is taking care of him, and Papa is there as well. He'll be safe, and he'll have a very sturdy cast to keep his arm from moving as it heals." As they walked, she looked back at her daughter. Drop was still pale, and her fingers were shaking. Anca frowned. Then, she crouched beside Drop and cupped her cheek. "Drop, do you feel like this is your fault?"

The girl shifted and scratched the back of her leg with her foot. Anca frowned. Her silence was speaking volumes, especially as she avoided Anca's gaze. After a moment, Anca stroked Drop's cheek. "My dearest, none of this is your fault; it was an accident. You didn't know he was going to fall, nor did you make him fall. It happened, it's over, and he will be alright."

"I said we should climb," Drop mumbled. She continued to avoid Anca's gaze, shifting once more and wiping her eyes. "I shouldn't have said we should climb."

Anca sighed and pulled her stepdaughter closer. The little girl began to cry, and Anca shut her eyes to savor the embrace. "Sh, you're alright, my love. It's not your fault. There is no fault to be had."

Drop didn't answer, prompting Anca to lift her and carry her home. Eventually, Drop's sniffles quieted and she leaned against Anca's shoulder. Little fingers played with curls that fell from Anca's bun, providing a breath of fresh air. It wasn't normal enough to pull her from her sorrow, but as she sat Drop down on the sofa and then cuddled quietly with her, she found that it was, perhaps, the most normal thing that had happened in a while. Whether or not that was a good thing, Anca had yet to decide. Still, she wrapped Drop in a blanket and held her close. Drop played with the quilt quietly, fiddling with the hem, before she looked at Anca with huge eyes. "Are you and Papa going to have a baby?"

It was such an innocent question, and Anca wanted to keep from crying as she stared at her daughter. She swallowed back tears. "Maybe. HaMelech will give us a baby if He decides it's time."

"Oh," Drop said back. She settled closer to Anca, silent for another moment. "I hope it's a little brother. I don't want a sister; then I have to share my dresses with her."

Anca couldn't help but laugh, wiping her eyes to mask her sorrow. "I'll keep that in mind, my love. It's a little hard to decide that on my own."

A hum answered Anca's words, and Drop cuddled closer. She didn't ask anymore questions, though Anca knew she was curious. The woman couldn't be upset with Drop, either. Curiosity was only natural, and when there were other families with small children, of course Drop would want to know.

After a little while, Anca and Drop started to bake the bread that Anca had left to rise. Shatter and Flick still hadn't returned, and Anca was growing concerned that it was more than a simple break. She did her best to distract herself and Drop, welcoming the addition of Rolandus and Olare. The two men frowned as she explained where Flick and Marin were, and sympathetic murmurs rang out about Shatter's arm.

Eventually, Rolandus patted Anca's shoulder. "He'll be alright; Marin is an excellent healer, and Flick has him settled, I'm sure."

Anca nodded a little bit. "I hope so. We'll wait for them to join us before we eat, regardless."

When the others joined, Shatter's arm was splinted to the elbow. He looked exhausted, and Flick laid him down in his box bed. "He's still needing to rest; they had to ensure he was completely asleep to tend to the breaks."

"It was that bad?" Anca asked.

Flick nodded, kissed her forehead, and looked towards the box bed. "Three breaks in one bone, the other bone completely snapped. He'll be alright, but it'll be a lengthy recovery."

He sighed quietly, prompting Anca to rub his back for a moment. When he gave her a tired smile, Anca wrapped her arms around him. He ran his fingers through her hair, closing his eyes as his shoulders sagged and he exhaled. Anca closed her eyes as well, simply resting in his arms. She had no doubt that he was struggling just as much as she was. Eventually, she pulled away, and Olare spoke from beside the fire.

"Do we need to leave for the evening?"

"No, no," Flick said. He pulled away from Anca, leaving her to tend to the rest of dinner, and sat heavily beside Rolandus and Olare.

Out of the corner of her eye, Anca watched him hang his head and the two men place hands on his back. While she couldn't hear them, she knew they were praying over her husband and all they were going through. Marin joined Anca after a little while— she had stayed to tidy the Temple where Shatter was tended to—and put her hand on Anca's shoulder. "How are you doing?"

"I'm alive," Anca murmured. She glanced at Drop, who was playing with her doll near the bedbox, and sighed. "Just trying to keep those two safe. It was hard to meet anyone's eye after Shatter's accident."

"It wasn't your fault, nor was it Drop's," Marin said quietly. "Those children are quite happy and safe; things like that happen when there are possibilities for injuries. It's a part of life, and a part of parenthood."

Anca turned to face her friend, frowning. "Drop asked if her father and I were going to have a baby together." She searched Marin's face, holding tightly to her apron again. Marin's eyes were wide, and Anca, after a moment, sighed. "I'm sorry, I... I'm exhausted from asking for a miracle. It's been a year and a half. You'd think that maybe, just maybe, something would work but...." Shaking her head, Anca began to ladle stew into bowls. "Regardless, I've got these two to keep watch over."

"Anca—"

"Can you please bring these to the men?" Anca interrupted.

She didn't want to speak any further about parenthood. The topic made her heart ache, and she was afraid that, if she spoke of it any sooner, she'd cry. Drop didn't need to see the tears, and she didn't want their friends to feel the need to worry. As Flick looked up from their prayer, he gestured for her to join him. Marin sat the bowls down and settled on the floor beside Rolandus. Anca did the same, finding Flick's hands resting on her head and shoulder. She sighed, looking down. Her husband, from above her, whispered, "We can't do this on our own, my love."

"Flick, I didn't want to involve anyone else," Anca breathed back. She bit her lip. Shame and guilt were beginning to swirl over her again, and her voice caught. "Please, I just want to eat and retire. I don't want to pray."

Flick paused at the words, and he slipped from his seat to embrace her tightly. It took a moment, but soon Anca began to cry, sobbing into his shoulder. Rolandus, Olare, and Marin moved closer, and Anca could hear their whispered prayers. They weren't prayers that asked for children, but prayers of peace and wisdom.

Anca settled in Flick's chest, shuddering as Marin's quiet voice rose over her. "Please, HaMelech, soothe their hearts in this season. You haven't abandoned them, You will bring them what they desire, and You will protect their hearts through this time. Thank you, HaMelech, for the blessings they have received and for the blessings that You shower over us daily. Shatter is safe, his arm will heal. Thank you for keeping him from a greater injury, and thank you for the parents that You've given him through Flick and Anca."

As the prayer died down, Anca leaned into Flick's side. He brushed over her hair again, passed out the stew, and they ate in silence. Rolandus and Olare began to discuss the happenings with the training knights, and Flick involved himself there. Anca and Marin listened politely, and then they transitioned to playing a handful of games of chess. The three visitors left well into the evening, and Anca excused herself to sleep. Flick didn't argue, though he followed her later.

As he pulled her near, Anca couldn't catch herself from whispering, "I'm sorry I can't complete our family."

"It isn't your fault, so you needn't apologize."

"I can't conceive, or carry."

"You've kept our children safe, that in itself is more than enough," Flick breathed back. He pressed his nose to her neck, sighed, and shifted. "Anca, our family is complete with or without a baby. I know I want another child as desperately as you do, but... If that isn't in HaMelech's will, then I suppose I will survive."

"You don't get it—"

"I understand far more than you think, my love," Flick said. Anca turned to face him, finding his dark eyes were sad. "I do not understand it in the same vein as you, but I know that my heart aches each time you tell me of your pain, of another loss, of nothingness. I'm here for you through this... but I wonder how long we should place ourselves into this painful cycle."

Anca turned away again, clinging to the blankets. She said nothing, instead beginning to cry, and did her best to keep quiet for the sake of their children. Flick, too, was silent as he clung to her.

Chapter Four

Three Years

Anca rested her head on her arms and wept.

She felt incredibly foolish for doing so while at work, but after dealing with the fourth dove who murmured that there wasn't any reason she wasn't conceiving, let alone missing her monthly courses, the emotions were simply too much to deal with. She shuddered as Marin put her hand on her back, then she wiped her face.

"Anca—"

"I don't know why it upsets me, still," Anca whispered, furiously beginning to redo her hair amid her tears. "I've got two children, nearly nine and eight years old; it'd be cruel to ask Flick to start over again."

"You've been married only three years," Marin said back. She crouched beside Anca, and the blonde looked away from her. She didn't want to see the sadness in Marin's face, not when she knew it would make her cry again. "I'm sure Flick would be ecstatic to raise a baby again."

Had it been that long already?

Anca thought over the last several years, sucking in a breath. It didn't seem like it'd been three years. Her children had been so small just yesterday, it seemed, but now they were becoming quite the young adults. Her eyes filled with tears. Drop and Shatter both had asked about a younger sibling recently. The women at church were asking again. Her coworkers brought it up. Everyone seemed to be talking about it, as desperately as Anca wanted to avoid the topic. She wiped at her eyes again, trying to ignore the voices echoing in her head.

"Maybe it's for the best; HaMelech might have done this."

That one was the worst. It was meant in love, but all Anca felt was bile rising in her throat. Yes, HaMelech might have willed this. He had willed other things before, such as sickness and justice, but the thought of someone using that truth in an attempt to comfort made Anca want to ball her fists up and scream into the sky.

Simply because it was true, didn't mean it brought comfort.

It had made Anca wrestle with the character of HaMelech for several weeks. He was a good and loving God, someone who lavished gifts upon His children and desired to bless them. The idea of putting someone through years of infertility and miscarriage seemed against who He was, and He couldn't act against who He was. Perhaps it was to protect her from something more? Anca wracked her brain. Perhaps the lack of courses was to keep her from miscarriage. If she couldn't conceive, she couldn't lose. It was a morbid thought, but it was a blessing in some regard. Anca inhaled and shook her head. "Marin?"

"Yes?"

"Remind me that I need to focus on everything else going on, not the heartbreak," Anca murmured. She straightened up, released her shaking breath, and wiped her face again. "You have three women you need to check in on today, and a couple of elderly patients as well. Housecalls, of course." Swallowing, Anca pulled out a small list with neatly written addresses and names on them. "You'll have one of the younger women with you today—I hadn't seen her name on rotations before, but I'm sure she'll be a great help."

Marin nodded and then paused. "I love how you say 'younger woman', Anca. She can't be much younger than you."

"I'm nearly twenty-four, practically in my grave." Anca brushed her hands over her documents, tucking things back into their pile as some of her hair fell over her eyes. "The way Drop has begun to pine after boys makes me worried for the next few years. Poor Flick is already going grey; he's not yet thirty, and he's going to be silver before we know it."

"Olare dyes his beard. Flick, I'm sure, can find something," Marin replied.

The two looked at each other and Anca, after a moment, couldn't help but begin to laugh. Flick would do his best to argue about the grey in his hair, she was sure. The thought of Olare dying his beard, too, was preposterous. Anca shook her head and smiled at her friend Marin was grinning, her own hair wild and falling from her bun. It took a moment, but then Anca smiled. "Thank you... I needed a laugh."

"Anytime, Anca."

Anca carefully finished tending to her desk as a courier came in. "Mrs. Alastar?"

"I am she."

"I have a letter... it's from 'Miss Jessica'?"

Anca frowned. "I'll take it, thank you." She took the letter from the young man and scanned it, one eyebrow raising. Then, in a flurry of movements, she scanned her ledger and sat back to rub the bridge of her nose. Marin tilted her head, silent. Finally, Anca sighed. "She can't come in. She's caught the measles."

"I knew it would spread through the town eventually," Marin said. She looked over Anca's desk. "Do you have anyone else who could help me?"

"No."

That wasn't true. Anca would be able to; her shift would end soon enough, but that then allowed for her to help her friend. Three of those cases, though, were women who were due to deliver children anyday. While Anca could do it, she had enough training as a midwife to return to assisting Marin in that endeavor, she wasn't sure she could aid anyone in the process after her own struggles. Then, guilt gnawed at her heart from the lie she told, and she stood up.

"Anca?"

"I'll go with you." Anca didn't look at the redhead as she exchanged her suit jacket for an apron, pinning her silver brooch of a dove in flight to her right breast. She pulled her hair into a tighter bun, rummaged under her desk for a handful of files, and handed them to Marin. "You'll need two sets of hands if these visits turn into a child birthing session, and I don't trust Mr. Anderson's tongue should you be alone."

She paused briefly to look at Marin, whose green eyes had softened in a matter of moments. Her friend was holding the papers quietly, watching her go from place to place, before she murmured, "I hope you know how much I admire you, Anca, and your desire to serve others."

"It's what HaMelech calls me to do," Anca said back. She pulled a hat onto her head and then flicked a little plaque onto her desk that said 'gone for lunch'. Then, as she gathered her bag, she took the files from Marin. "Let's go; time doesn't wait for us."

The two made their way from the Temple of HaMelech and through the sleepy village of Apple Ridge. It was a beautiful day, despite all that Anca was going through, and she allowed herself the pleasure of sightseeing as they walked. It was a welcome change from tending to others, to her stepchildren, or helping Flick from the garden. She sucked in a breath. Perhaps this was the season she would stay in for many years. Perhaps HaMelech was simply asking her to walk and enjoy the beauty of the world.

Deep in the pit of her stomach, Anca truly hoped that it was only a season, and that it would pass.

She and Marin stopped at a small house where Mr. Anderson, one of the oldest inhabitants of Apple Ridge resided, and then knocked. From inside, a little grunt answered them. Anca glanced at Marin. "HaMelech help us; he sounds like he's in a bad mood."

Marin chuckled softly. "He's been in a bad mood the last two times, poor thing... this is perhaps the best answer I've gotten."

Anca smiled a little as they slipped into the building, Marin going first. "Mr. Anderson, it's Marin and Anca from the Temple of HaMelech. We're just here to check on your breathing and administer your medicines if needed."

"Eh... I'm fine," came the stern reply. It was followed by a barking cough, making Anca wince, before a little sigh rang out. "Fine, get it over with."

Mr. Anderson was laying on his bed, propped up as he hacked into a cloth. Marin set her bag on the rickety table and carefully turned the gas lamp on, casting a light over the dark room. Anca stared at the man, and her shoulders sagged slightly. There was a smell rising from his bed, not that of bodily fluid or rot, but a solid smell that made her stomach curl and her skin crawl. She looked at Marin, who was beginning to quietly draw medicines into her syringe, before she looked at Mr. Anderson. "How long have you been in bed, sir?"

"Can't hardly walk anymore," he said, glaring towards her. "The cough makes me fall."

Anca nodded to herself and looked at Marin. Her friend was beginning to notice the smell, too, and she tilted her head at Mr. Anderson. "Has anyone been able to wash your bedding, or tend to your dishes?

His glare snapped towards her. "What do you think, missy?"

As Marin straightened up, Anca thanked HaMelech that her friend was level-headed. "Let us strip the bed for you, then, and we'll wash it. Sleeping in this bed will do nothing for your health if the bedding isn't tended to, and the rotting food from your dishes will encourage rodents." Mr. Anderson's glare didn't fade, but he eventually sighed and nodded.

It was the form of a man who had given up, and expected others to do the same. He was lonely, sick, and the facade of being tough was rapidly fading as Anca and Marin began to help him from his bed and into a seat. His first step made him cling to Anca's arm, and she murmured a quiet encouragement as he shuffled to the chair and heavily sat down.

Then, Anca began to strip the bed sheets as Marin worked on dishes. This was more than they would often be asked to do, but Anca knew it wouldn't take too long to finish this task and hire a washerwoman to finish cleaning the bedding for her. They put new sheets on the bed, helped Mr. Anderson back in, and went on their way as soon as the bedding was sorted.

Marin was quiet, finally broaching the subject as she murmured, "You don't think he has long, do you?"

"No, Marin," Anca said gently. She rubbed Marin's back, watching her older friend quietly, before she said, "He'll be at peace once he passes... but I don't think he'll be with us for much longer. His body is fading, though I don't think it's time to give him that prognosis. Tomorrow, if he isn't doing better, we will have that conversation. Today, we pray that HaMelech's will be done."

They continued to their other appointments, speaking with other patients and checking pregnancies quietly. Anca's hands shook as she carefully felt an expecting mother's belly, feeling the baby within roll and kick. It was a good sign; the child was healthy, and its mother wasn't in pain. Anca smiled a little as she looked at the other woman. "I think you're doing just fine. You're measuring right on time, and the baby is moving well. Have you been dealing with any headaches, swelling, or bleeding?"

Her patient shook her head, prompting Marin to scribble a few notes, and Anca smiled. "Good; those are all symptoms that I need you to watch for, as well as if your baby moves. Ten times per hour, now, alright? If the baby moves less, try moving around, drinking some cold water, or bathing. If even that doesn't work, you'll need to come to the Temple and we'll see what's going on."

Again, she received a nod, and Anca turned away as Marin took over. She sucked in a breath, doing her best to keep from crying as Marin covered how labor would work once it began. She hadn't thought that this conversation would trigger more tears, much less in front of a stranger.

It wasn't until they were returning to the Temple that Marin stopped Anca and took her hands. "How are you doing?"

"Do you want the truth?" Anca asked, beginning to look anywhere outside of Marin's face. "Or would you like the safe answer?"

"I want the truth, Anca."

Releasing a shaking breath, Anca hung her head. How was she doing? Truthfully, Anca desperately wanted to cry and ask HaMelech why she was being tempted in this way. She wanted to scream, wail, and make a scene to try and bring some fruition of blessing to her. She wanted Flick to be a father to a child shared between them, but she was terrified to try for a child when there had been no monthly courses, and so no hope for a child to form in her womb. She didn't want to ache, yet she worked with families joyously welcoming children.

It scared Anca doing so; the last thing she wanted to do was curse those who received blessings when she didn't. An inability to praise HaMelech for blessings that He gave to others showed that she was not yet ready to fully receive blessings of her own. It was a heart issue. How much of it was a heart issue in its entirety, rather than a medical issue?

"I'm hurt, and scared, and... I'm afraid I'm growing bitter."

Marin squeezed her hands and Anca shook her head. She didn't want reassurance. She didn't like the idea of Marin trying to comfort her about the future. As she stood with the redhead, Anca found herself in a tight hug. Marin didn't say anything, and neither did Anca, as they held onto each other.

Eventually, Anca pulled away and wiped her eyes again. "I should get home; the children will be getting out of school soon, and I need to get dinner ready."

"Anca?"

She paused and Marin searched her face. "I love you, and I hope you know that we are all praying for you."

"I don't need pity, Marin," Anca whispered.

"It isn't pity. It's a genuine desire for HaMelech to move and reveal His plan," Marin corrected softly. "My heart breaks for you, especially when you aid me with these calls. It was an incredibly hard day, I'm sure, and I am so proud of you for being willing to serve even in this moment."

Anca wiped her eyes. "How could I not serve?" she asked. "Marin, I haven't anything but what HaMelech has provided. Flick and I have nothing from Zanther aside from ourselves and the children. HaMelech has given me everything, at the very least I can give Him my obedience."

Marin smiled at her, wiped some tears from her cheeks, and gave her another hug. Anca clung to her, closing her eyes, before she pulled away. "I'll see you tomorrow."

She looked at her shoes as she walked, hurrying home to remove her apron and brooch before she started to tidy the sitting area and chop vegetables. Flick would be home soon, too, from working with Rolandus and Olare. She put it in the back of her mind: she needed to speak to him about what they were going to do.

Drop and Shatter arrived home soon enough. Anca kissed their heads as they entered, watched them place their lunch pails beside the hearth, and then received two hugs. Drop was growing quickly; she was nearly as tall as Anca was, though that wasn't a hard feat to do, and she had become quite the young lady in a short amount of time. Anca smiled as she studied Drop's curls, squeezed her again, and held her for a moment. Though there wasn't any blood relation, Anca was sad that her daughter was getting so old, so fast.

She moved her attention to Shatter, who was getting tall, too. His eyes sparkled mischievously as she hugged him tightly, closing her eyes as she stroked his inky black hair. He was nearly a spitting image of Flick, down to the quirk of his lips that never seemed to leave. Anca brushed some of his hair from his face and kissed his forehead. "You both had a good day, yes?"

It was usually a good report. They were well behaved, and Flick ensured that their behavior, though they were in Apple Ridge rather than Zanther, was fitting their last name.

Alastar.

Anca frowned to herself before she shook her head. It was such a prestigious name in Zanther, and they left it behind. They were making a new path, one that Flick had so carefully forged for them after they escaped the cold prisons. Only one other carried that name, and that was the High Inquisitor Fernando Alastar... Flick's father. They had no tie to him, not after what he had done. They wouldn't claim to have tie, either; the children had been so young when their torture occurred, and so, Anca didn't bring it up.

"Mostly." Shatter looked away from Anca and Drop, from beside the hearth, shifted.

"Mostly?" Anca repeated, looking between them. "What do you mean by 'mostly'?"

Neither of her stepchildren looked at her, and so she simply stared. Drop continued to shift in her discomfort as Shatter crossed his arms over his chest. Still, even as she waited, nothing came from them. Finally, Anca murmured, "Both of you, sit on the sofa until your father gets home. I have given you time to answer me as to what has happened, and you will not."

"Yes, Mother," Drop murmured.

Shatter simply nodded and sat beside his sister.

Anca frowned at them, shook her head, and continued to make supper. Out of the corner of her eye, she watched as Drop murmured something to Shatter, who then shook his head furiously.

What on torus could they have done that they wouldn't admit to her? They hadn't stolen, had they? Lying was wrong, too, but she couldn't believe that either of them would lie. Perhaps they were omitting the truth for a different reason?

Anca rubbed her Temples. The house was silent until Flick arrived from work, his hair slicked back and dirt coating his face. He kissed Anca lightly, ruffled Drop and Shatter's hair, and began to wash his face with the cool water. "Good evening, everyone! It's good to be home. Was work alright today, dear?"

"Yes, it was," Anca said lightly. "I went with Marin on her rounds today; one of our doves has caught the measles, so that's going around."

"Measles? Again?" Flick looked at her, his brow knit. "I suppose it was a good thing we caught it several months ago, then... How was school, children?"

Anca watched their children, one eyebrow raised, as they looked at each other again. Then, Flick looked at her, and she shook her head. "I've had them wait to speak to you. Shatter said they had a mostly good day, but I've yet to hear what that meant. They were awfully quiet while sitting here, too."

She leaned against the wall as Flick frowned and crossed to them. Then, he crouched before them and looked at them. "In this home, we serve HaMelech, correct?"

"Yes, Father," Drop murmured. Shatter nodded.

"And HaMelech commands children to obey their parents, correct? Just as He commands that we teach our children in His ways and do not provoke you to anger?"

Again, the children nodded at Flick, and he looked at Anca. One hand was outstretched to her and she took it, standing beside him as he looked back to the children. "Your mother asked what you meant; you did not answer, nor did you explain anything, from what I understand. Is this correct?"

"Yes," Shatter mumbled.

"You will both be receiving a consequence for disobeying her. I expect you to answer her when she asks you to explain, even if that results in asking to wait for me." Flick squeezed Anca's hand and then looked between them. "What happened if you only 'mostly' had a good day?"

It took a few moments more before either Drop or Shatter spoke. When they did, Anca held tighter to Flick's hand.

"Shatter got into a fight, as did I," Drop finally said quietly.

"Why? We don't solve anything with violence if we can avoid it." Flick frowned. "What happened?"

Anca sank down to look at their children. There were bruises forming under Drop's eye and around Shatter's knuckles. Her eyes softened and she brushed over their injuries. Why hadn't she noticed those? Guilt flooded Anca, and she kissed their heads. Flick glanced at her, opening his mouth to ask her why, but Shatter interrupted.

"Someone said Mother was barren, and that you were going to leave her, and just... all sorts of horrible things," he said quietly. He looked up at them, tears in his eyes. "I told them to stop, but they didn't. So I hit them. And... and Drop got involved because she tried to help, and they said that she was a half-breed because we don't share a mother and..."

Flick stood abruptly. "Who were they?"

"Flick, please, don't make a big deal out of what started it. I want them to receive consequences for what they said about Drop and Shatter, but..."

Flick grabbed Anca's arms and she stared up at him.

She didn't flinch. She knew that his anger, even in this capacity, was directed with a righteous desire to correct a wrong. It wasn't towards her, but those who desired to gossip, sow dissension, and otherwise turn from the love that HaMelech had given them. He held her tightly and Anca, after a moment, whispered, "Our children are the most precious thing we have, and I don't want anyone else to speak of them the way they did today. I've dealt with this since we married; I can get over it. Please, only speak to the parents about what was said about Drop and Shatter, not me."

It took him a moment before he nodded, pulled on his cloak, and gestured to the children. "Come with me; I'm still not pleased that you resorted to violence. I am, however, proud of you for standing up for one another, and for your mother."

They left and Anca sunk onto the couch. She offered a quiet prayer to HaMelech, thanking Him for the tenderness that Flick showed their children and a prayer of forgiveness for the children involved... as well as their parents.

Her family returned an hour later and they sat for a silent dinner. It wasn't until the children retired for bed that she leaned into her husband and finally cried, the stress of the day settling over her. "Why are they so horrible? Flick, I can't stand for it! The gossip, the rumors, the hateful words! How are we to move past it if people in this town continue to beat this to the ground?"

Flick sighed and Anca tightened her grip. He wasn't going to break down, she knew that. He was stoic, carefully weighing each word and comparing it to what the Holy Texts said. She loved that about him; he did his best to follow HaMelech's words even in the midst of pain. Part of her hated it, though. She disliked the logic that he held tightly to when she needed emotion. Still, there was nothing more that she could desire than his heart to follow the King of Kings.

As she thought, he murmured, "We will continue to pray to Him, and we will ask Him to strengthen us so we can forgive them." He was quiet for a long moment before he sighed and shook his head. "I don't know what else to do, Anca."

He didn't often admit that. He did his best to seem like he knew what to do, to keep their family from faltering in the face of hardships, but now Anca could see the exhaustion that had begun to set in. She looked up at him to see that his face was stricken with concern and tears had filled his eyes. Anca reached up to brush his cheek and he leaned into her hand.

"I love you," he whispered, sighing heavily once more. "I love you dearly, Anca and... and I pray that I can take all of this pain, all of this sadness, and all of this waiting from you. But we both know I can't. In fact, the only thing I can do is pray to HaMelech that things will change." He opened his eyes to look at her, searching her face. Anca knew he had heard that she broke down in the Temple. She had no doubt that the whispers in the town had sent him news that she was struggling yet again. It was constant, and she wished nothing more than to finally have a day where she could be encouraged and celebrate with Flick, rather than for others.

It wasn't their time, though, and she wasn't sure if it would be.

"I want to have a child with you, Anca," Flick mumbled. "I worry that maybe, just maybe, HaMelech has it in His plan that we as a family are complete. I pray that His will allows for that child but..."

"It isn't our will to enact," Anca said back. She sighed, offered a sad smile, and looked at her husband. He was stroking tears away from her face again, and he quietly kissed her forehead as she said, "I trust HaMelech, as saddened as I am. I know that He has a plan, and... and He is good, even if this doesn't seem good. We'll be alright... right?"

"Always; He's a good God."

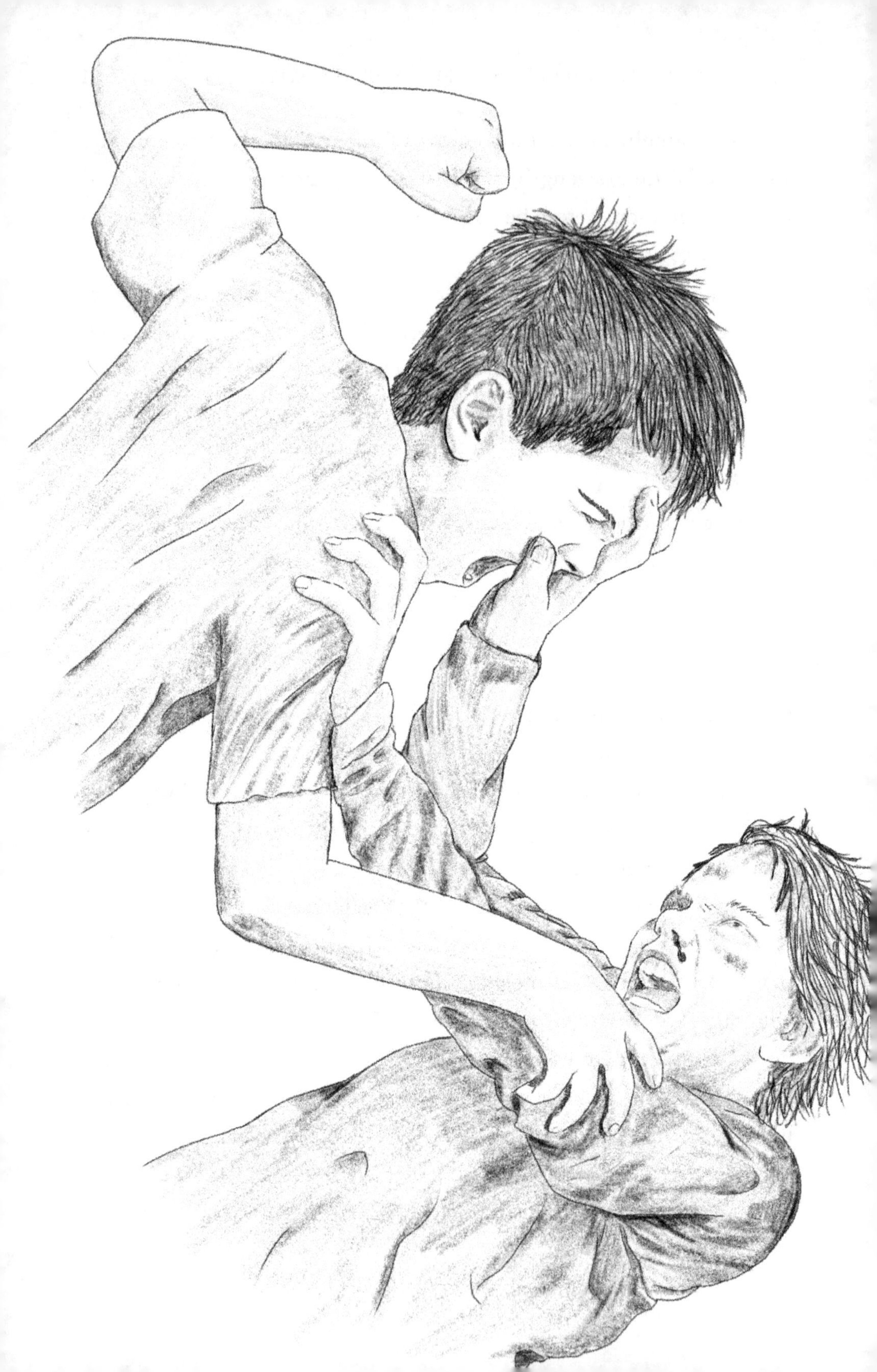

Chapter Five

Four and a Half Years

Anca watched as Flick straightened up, his hand raised. "In the name of HaMelech, I swear to serve as a captain of the Knights of the Long Road. I will protect travelers, regardless of their beliefs, enact justice with a tender heart, and continue life as a faithful follower of our King." His eyes flickered to her and she smiled at him from beside their children, nodding slightly. He smiled back, his shoulders relaxing ever so slightly before his gaze returned to Olare.

Their friend was standing before him, his face hard though Anca knew he was pleased. He'd been pushing for Flick to accept the position of a captain for a year, and, finally, Flick had accepted. Anca had been praying for his decision, too, as she wasn't sure what HaMelech wanted for them. There were so many choices, and Flick had desperately wanted to ensure they were fulfilling HaMelech's will and not their own.

Beside her, Drop and Shatter shifted in their nice clothes. The two looked up at her, and she gave them a bit of a nod. They were growing bored; Anca couldn't rightly blame them, as this was a long ceremony to watch for a nine and ten year old.

Marin lightly nudged Anca and gestured towards Flick with her chin. Anca followed her gaze, beginning to smile as she watched Olare pin a medal to Flick's chest and then salute. Flick saluted in kind before they embraced. Clapping erupted through the Temple, and Anca, followed by their children, stood to applaud. Flick turned to look at them, beaming, and then made his way down the steps. He pulled Drop and Shatter in for a hug and then hugged Anca tightly. She pressed her face into his chest, closed her eyes, and held tightly to him.

This meant more responsibilities; he would be able to lead groups now, and that meant he was more likely to serve in Bleak Hollow than he had been before. Those were long trips, dangerous ones, at that, and brought him towards Zanther again.

Anca tightened her grip, inhaled, and murmured, "I'm proud of you."

"I'm proud of you," he whispered back. "You're such a brave woman, and I'm so grateful for your support."

She nodded against his chest and pulled away, offering him a little smile.

The celebration for his promotion moved well into the night, culminating in a dance before each family retired. Anca sank onto the sofa beside Flick and sighed, resting her feet on a small table that he had painstakingly made for her. He kissed her head and rested a hand on her leg. "Tired?"

"Exhausted." Anca smiled at him, searching his face quietly. "I didn't expect there to be this much of a party."

"Olare and Rolandus started it," Flick laughed. "I wouldn't expect less!"

They sat together for several moments in silence as Flick carefully fixed his feathered mantle and Anca began to darn some of Shatter's socks. Then, Flick looked at her.

"How is your heart doing, my love?"

"My heart?"

"We haven't spoken of expanding our family as of late," Flick said gently. He searched her face, making Anca look away. "Are you doing alright?"

Was she?

Anca slowly lowered her work. She had done her best to forget about that desire. Her courses had yet to return, and she had tried desperately to push the reminder of anything to do with the topic away. As she sighed, Flick put a hand on her leg and she looked at him. She did her best to smile, though it didn't reach her eyes. Still, as her husband shifted closer and pulled her into his arms, Anca allowed herself to exhale again and relax. He was here to love her, he was here to support her. As she sat, Flick began to stroke her hair. "Can I pray with you?"

"Please," Anca whispered.

There was nothing else to do in this situation. She was going to mourn what could have been, even if there was something she could cling to. Hope was fleeting in her mind, though, and she sighed and she closed her eyes.

Flick put his hand on her belly. "HaMelech, Father, thank you for Anca. Thank you for my beautiful bride of nearly five years; her heart is tender for our children, and she is so incredibly gentle with our patients. I can see love for others each day, and I'm amazed each morning that You have brought her to my side. Thank you. Thank you for our children, Drop and Shatter. When they were named, there was bitterness and sorrow in my heart towards the situation, but now I see that rather than tears dropping down my face, and my heart shattered in my chest, You have brought me a drop of dew that returns each morning as a promise of Your faithfulness, and You have shattered my former life and made it into something so beautiful. Thank you... thank you for all of Your blessings."

He was quiet for a moment and Anca put her hand on his own. Then, as tenderly as she'd ever heard him, Flick whispered, "Father...

please... we ask for a miracle. Anca..." His voice caught and he took her hand, shaking now as he whispered, "We are heartbroken and don't understand your plan. Please... we ask for Your hand of healing on Anca's body, on her womb, that she may conceive. We pray for Your blessings over the child You have prepared for us... and we ask, more than anything, that You comfort us as we wait in this season of anxiety and confusion. Help us to trust Your perfect plan, and help us to lean into You, even when we don't understand Your ways."

He murmured his soft 'amen' and Anca echoed it, though she didn't say much more.

It was all she could do to keep from crying as she sat there, her husband's rhythmic stroking of her hair beginning to lull her into sleep.

When she awoke, stiff from laying on the sofa, she found that Flick was snoring softly beneath her. She smiled slightly at the sight and kissed his forehead before she slowly stood. There were still things to be done, even as night loomed around them and time marched on. Quietly, Anca prepared a loaf of bread for the morning before she pulled on her shawl and took a midnight walk.

The town of Apple Ridge was safe; it was perhaps one of her favorite things about the village, as the fortified walls ensured that chitters and other threats remained outside. It did block the view of the apple orchards unless one perched on the hill overlooking the entirety of Apple Ridge, and that view in itself was dizzyingly breathtaking. Anca decided to make her way towards the hill. The stars would be shining brightly above her, providing a clear space to look up and to think.

When she arrived, she sank down to the ground and then leaned back. The tree's leaves didn't block her whole view, allowing her to stare into space with a sigh.

How incredibly small she was there, watching falling stars and the little lights twinkle out.

Part of Anca wondered if, because she was so small, HaMelech heard her prayers. There were so many others on Illeross, people she knew and those she didn't, that He was constantly watching and providing for. It was strange to think that maybe, just maybe, he heard her too. The Holy Texts did stay He was everywhere, though, and she knew those were true. There was no way that the day in the forest with Marin, nearly five years ago, was simply a spectacle. Something had been there.

Something, or rather, someone, heard.

Slowly, Anca inhaled as she watched the stars. "Please."

They twinkled above her, and she sighed.

"HaMelech, help my unbelief... if it's a heart issue you're working on, then please, give me a sign. Give me some whisper, something that reassures me."

Again, Anca sighed and closed her eyes. She was tired. She was so incredibly tired of hoping only to find sorrow. Four and a half years brought that about, and she worried about Flick every bit as much as she worried for herself. There was a lot of responsibility on him now. It came from the new position, alongside running the household, and raising their children. Guilt flooded Anca, and she sighed. The children were so incredibly loving amid the mourning, too. She knew she had done her best to keep them from seeing her sadness, but children knew; they were much smarter than most people assumed. Anca sighed, closed her eyes, and lost herself to thought.

***

She was awoken rather rudely by shaking, and she batted the hands away before she was suddenly enveloped in arms. However it was shaking, sobbing as she was held, and she opened her eyes to find inky black hair obscuring her vision.

When the embrace was broken, she found that it was Flick. He stroked her cheeks, searching her face, before he turned away. "Marin! Marin, I've found her!

"Flick...?"

"I woke and you were gone! The door was unlocked, there was no sign of you anywhere!" Flick pulled her back into his arms and shook his head. "When did you leave? Why didn't you return?"

Anca stared at him before her eyes widened. "Flick... oh, Flick, I'm so sorry! I had come out to think, and I meant to return after..." She trailed off and looked around, taking in the crushed grass from her rest before she rubbed her forehead. "I'm so sorry. Did you think...?"

"I didn't know what to think," Flick admitted. He helped her stand and held her to his side. Anca found that her legs were incredibly stiff as she walked, so she leaned into Flick in order to keep from falling. Her husband helped her down the hill and to Marin, who had raced to them as soon as she saw them. Flick lightly waved her off. "She's okay as far as I can tell."

"I left for a walk, and I was just going to think but..." Anca trailed off and hung her head. Marin put a hand on Acna's arm, stooping down to look at her face. Then, as Anca met her eyes, she looked back at Flick.

"May I bring her to the Temple, Flick?" she finally asked softly.

Anca looked up at her husband, whose eyes flickered to her quickly. He searched her face. "Did you want to go with Marin, or would you like to go back home?" He squeezed her lightly. "If Marin thinks you should go to the Temple, then please feel free to do so."

"I don't... know," Anca whispered. As she stood there, she suddenly became aware of her head beginning to swim and her hands beginning to shake. Flick held her a little tighter and looked at her face.

"My love?"

She didn't answer as she grabbed his tunic, swallowing as she clung to him. Flick lowered her to the ground and held her. "Anca, can you hear me?"

Again, Anca didn't respond as she began to tremble and gasp. It hurt to breathe. It hurt to move, it hurt to lay there. She stared at her husband, swallowing hard as he cupped his face and looked to Marin, before she felt her eyes flutter and her vision faded.

***

Waking up was hard, though she could hear Flick and Marin speaking to her. It sounded as though they were speaking through a bubble, and she desperately wanted to move towards them. She couldn't though, and that frightened her.

"Oh, Anca," Marin's voice breathed. "You're okay, sweetheart. It's alright, come to our voices."

Anca wanted to, desperately.

No matter what she tried to do, though, she couldn't seem to be able to force her eyes open.

"Anca," Flick murmured. There was a touch, somewhere, and Anca exhaled at the familiar feeling. Flick was beside her, he must have taken her hand. It would have soothed her, if she knew why she was lying so incredibly still. "Anca, my love. I need you to open your eyes. Please... please, my love, I need you to open your eyes and look at me."

How incredibly infuriating this was. Anca wanted nothing more than to scream, cry, something, to show them that she could hear them.

Flick sighed above her. "Marin... how long...?"

"I don't know if she'll be able to do it for another three days," Marin murmured. "We only have so many things we can do, so many procedures, to keep her from... from..."

Another heavy sigh answered Marin and Flick brushed over Anca's hair. "Alright."

Three days? No, that couldn't be right. It couldn't have been three days since she had to lay down, since she was on the hill. That had to be wrong.

HaMelech, why? Anca asked silently, though her voice made no words. Why allow this to happen? What purpose is there?

To know My grace is sufficient, came the still, soft answer.

Anca would have frowned if she was able, but instead she resigned herself to the silence. It was the only thing she had to cling to aside from HaMelech now, and that, in itself, scared her.

Flick remained by her side for a while, but she still wasn't sure that time had passed at all. Eventually, she felt his hand leave her and she found herself alone in the darkness once more.

***

Eventually, she heard Rolandus and Olare's voices above her. Flick was back, too, and they spoke quietly of Flick's deployment to Bleak Hollow. As desperately as Anca wanted to tell him that he had to obey the calling, and that this was what he promised to do, she was unable to do so. "I can't leave her," Flick said softly. "I can't leave the children, either. What sort of husband and father would I be to leave them at this time?"

"I can always watch Drop and Shatter," Marin said in return. I've not been called to Bleak Hollow, so I will be here."

"I appreciate it, but..." Flick sighed. "I don't know."

Olare's voice broke the silence, as commanding as ever. Anca was grateful for his presence in Flick's life, even more so as he simply said,

"Then you must pray. HaMelech desires to speak to us, and I have no doubts that He has a plan."

For a moment, his words hung in the air before crying took their place. A weight sank beside Anca again and she realized that it was Flick. She could feel Rolandus, Marin, and Olare growing closer to her bed, and their voices raised in soft prayer.

Do you trust Me? the soft voice questioned again, nothing more than a whisper. Anca, My grace is enough to cover you. Do you trust your family to Me, as frightened of doing so as you are?

I want to, Anca thought. I truly do.

Nothing came, and finally Flick whispered, "I will go to Bleak Hollow as HaMelech called me to do."

Anca was alone again outside of Marin's quiet voices and the visits Drop and Shatter made. Both children stayed beside her as often as they could aside from schooling, and Anca, uncertain of how much time had passed, leaned into the presence of HaMelech that remained.

***

Eventually, Flick returned. He took her hands again and Anca, to herself, smiled. They were calloused and rough, testament to the service he gave in Bleak Hollow as he fought against chitters. Part of her wondered if he had even gone home, or if he had come straight to her side. She hadn't heard his weapon on the floor, so it was likely outside or left in the care of Rolandus.

"I'm home," he breathed.

"I missed you," Anca mumbled back. It surprised her to hear her own voice, especially as raw and rasping as it was. As Flick startled, she knew that he, too, was surprised.

"Anca? Anca, my love? Can you hear me?"

She swallowed and nodded, ever so slightly, yet her eyes refused to open.

Flick took her hand again and she smiled. He continued to whisper to her, trying to coax her into looking at him, and then Marin's voice entered the room. "Flick, is she alright?"

"She spoke, Marin! She spoke, she could hear me! Marin, she's back!"

"Really? Oh, Flick! Anca, Anca, you're doing wonderfully! I'm so proud of you!"

It was a slow move to open her eyes, but eventually Anca managed to crack them open just enough to stare at her husband. His usually clean-shaven face had grown a short beard, and exhaustion rimmed his eyes as he expectantly searched her eyes. He cupped her face with his hand, tears streaking down his face. "My love..."

"Hi," she whispered back.

Flick kissed her hand and she sighed, closing her eyes again. "Get some rest, Anca. You need it... you're back, oh, praise HaMelech you're back!"

***

Slowly, over what felt like hours, Anca opened her eyes completely to look at her husband, and then sat up with his help. He sat behind her, stroking her hair as Marin removed a tube that ran down her throat. Anca coughed and hacked, but as her friend gave a reassuring smile, she couldn't help but smile in return. Eventually, as she rested against her husband, Marin murmured, "We weren't sure you were going to wake up."

"What happened?" Anca rasped, coughing again.

Marin glanced at Flick. "I... we don't have an answer. I thought it might have been an infection, but we could be wrong. All I know is that..."

"That?" Anca whispered.

Flick held her a little tighter. "I was gone for a month and a half, my love... you were asleep for nearly two." He was beginning to shake as Anca leaned into him, and he sucked in a breath. "I should have stayed—"

"No... HaMelech said... go." Anca shook her head and closed her eyes. "You... obeyed."

***

Her recovery was slow, and she despised it. Gone were her days spent traveling with Marin from home to home as a dove healer. She couldn't stand very long, either, without having a fainting spell; the first instance scared Flick half to death, as he came home to find her laying beside the kitchen table. Anca spent most of her time sitting either on the sofa or outside of their home, darning socks or watching Drop and Shatter work in the garden.

Thank HaMelech for her children!

Drop and Shatter had taken up many of the responsibilities Anca had been in charge of. Each night, Anca patiently taught Drop how to make dinner or finish a stitch in her needlework. Shatter took up the garden when he was done with school, and he spent any free time working on sword play with Olare.

The community, the small family they foraged, banded tightly around them. Olare and Rolandus often helped Shatter gather firewood for their home, doing their best alongside Flick to help the young man grow into a responsible member of the household. Marin stayed to wash dishes on nights that Drop went to bed early, and Anca was often pleasantly surprised by a fresh pie or cookies that Marin had made for her.

Whispers didn't stop, but Anca found that, in remaining home outside of worship, it provided less of a chance for people to talk about her. All the while, she did her best to find peace in the situation. HaMelech's grace was sufficient; He had a plan, and it would go through regardless of her ability to do much.

***

Eventually, Anca looked at Flick and their children. She sighed, shook her head, and murmured, "I cannot begin to thank you for all you've done while I'm ill."

"Why wouldn't we?" Shatter asked incredulously. "Mamma, you took care of us a lot when we were sick."

Anca smiled slightly and took his hand. He was going to be taller than her any day now. She really couldn't believe how quickly he had grown. "Thank you, my love. And you too, Drop."

"Of course, Mother."

Drop smiled at Anca, so incredibly similar to her father while being completely different. Anca's eyes softened and she stroked Drop's cheek gently, smiling as her stepdaughter leaned into her touch. "I love you both so incredibly much." Flick's hand rested on her leg under the table and she looked at him. "I love you, too."

"Our family wouldn't be complete without you," Flick said softly.

Anca's smile faltered ever so slightly, but then she nodded. "It's perfect."

Chapter Six

Six Years

Six years.

Anca's fainting hadn't gotten any better, and she was more and more exasperated with her health continuing to decline. Flick and the children were wonderful, and that was perhaps her only saving grace.

There still was no diagnosis. Marin suggested doing various treatments for low blood pressure, as well as activities that could help her, but Anca had all but given up. Despite her frustrations, however, she did her best to cling to HaMelech's promise. His grace was sufficient, after all. He had her covered, as He always did.

Anca offered a weak smile to Flick as Marin checked her blood pressure, and then she sighed as Marin shook her head. "It's normal now, Anca."

"Of course, it is," Anca murmured back. Flick squeezed her hand slightly and she glanced at him. "I'm sorry. I didn't think that some gardening would cause a flare-up."

"You'd been able to beforehand," Flick replied. He kissed her forehead before he helped Anca to sit up. She swayed in his arms and caught herself, shaking her head at Flick's concerned look. Then, she glanced at Marin. "Easy does it, I assume?"

"Unfortunately, that's all I can really say."

As Anca and Flick left the Temple, she clung to his hand. His worried eyes never left her, and she offered him a little smile. "I'll be alright."

"I know... I'm still concerned," Flick said.

They gave one another a quiet smile before they reached their home, where a rather bored looking courier sat on the step. His little hat hung in one hand while his other propped up his head. There was a small trail of ants marching past him as he watched, each carrying a fragment of what Anca assumed was Shatter's hastily packed lunch, towards wherever they had set up their home. As Anca and Flick approached, the courier looked up, back at the ants, and then at them again. "Oh!" He fumbled to his feet, brushed off his rumpled shirt, and dug through his pack. "Are you... Anca... Cassy?"

For a moment, Anca stared. She hadn't gone by her maiden name since she and Flick were first married, and the only people who would remember that maiden name were people from Zanther. How they would have gotten where she lived, though, was incredibly strange. She didn't share that information, not after their escape from Zanther. It had been too dangerous to even think about it, especially with Flick's father still looking for them. Still, Anca shifted. "I am."

"Anca—" Flick began, but she looked at him.

"Good! I thought the others in town were crazy. They said there wasn't an Anca Cassy, but there was an Anca Alastar, but even then..." The courier brandished a letter towards them, beaming proudly. "I knew I'd find you!"

"And if you didn't?" Flick questioned.

Anca gave him a look as the courier grinned. "It would have gone up to Blackrock! This letter's been everywhere between Zanther and here!"

Doing her best to tune Flick and the courier out, Anca opened the letter and scanned it.

The first line had a script that she'd recognize anywhere. "It's from Adriata."

She glanced at Flick, who abandoned his conversation with the courier to look at her. One eyebrow raised, and she shook her head at him before she returned her gaze to the letter in her hands. As she did, she realized she was beginning to shake again. Flick caught her arm and held her. Then, after a moment, she looked at him. "She wants to visit," she whispered. "It's been six years and... and she wants to come and see me."

Once more, she looked at the letter in her hands and released a slow breath. After so long, it should have been a relief that her sister finally wanted to see her. On the other hand, she knew that Adriata had been incredibly hurt realizing that not only had Anca married Flick, but she had also decided to follow HaMelech rather than Solaris. It had been the last time she saw her older sister, and Anca knew there were likely a multitude of emotions that Adriata was experiencing on her end. As for Anca... the worries of what Adriata might bring to the peaceful town of Apple Ridge scared her. Releasing another breath, Anca slowly entered their home as Flick followed.

"Are you going to write back?"

"I want to," Anca said, sitting on the sofa. "I haven't seen her since..."

"Is it wise?" He replied, pacing before her. "Anca, Adriata was last employed by the inquisitors to act as eyes and ears in your hamlet—"

"You needn't remind me." Anca glanced at him. "I put that all together years ago, and assumed it was your idea at the time."

Stopping, Flick rubbed the back of his neck. Anca sighed to herself. It was a sore topic, she knew. As much as she disliked talking about the persecution they faced in Zanther, it was even harder to speak about the period in which Flick had lied to her about who he really was. She knew HaMelech had made him a new creation, but it was always a point that needed to be reconciled. As Flick returned to pacing, Anca shook her head. "I know it's dangerous, but... Flick, I miss her. That has to account for something, doesn't it?"

She watched Flick move back and forth, his arms behind his back as he thought. She was accustomed to this, keeping a close eye on him while waiting for his answer. Finally, he glanced at her. "She hates me. I don't trust that she's willing to be cordial if it means getting back at me for taking you into my home."

"She never had a chance to know who you were," Anca countered. "HaMelech will protect us, will he not? He always has, and He is faithful."

Her husband nodded, ran a hand through his hair, and looked at her. "They're going to go through her mail as soon as it enters Zanther. How do you propose letting her know that we're here?"

She hadn't figured that out, yet. But, after a moment, Anca met his eyes. "We send it with one of your patrols entering Zanther. They drop it off at the postmaster's, which will remove some eyes from it. I'll be careful with what I write, especially in ensuring that they don't know that you're with me. For the sake of correspondence, I can go by Anca Cassy; though the inquisitors know a lot, I doubt your father—" Flick grimaced, and she corrected herself, "I doubt the High Inquisitors have viewed our marriage as binding. Besides, last I was aware, they're only looking for Flick Alastar and the witch he decided to be involved with. He didn't care to ask for my name, remember?"

"He didn't care for anything but making himself look better," her husband returned dryly. After a moment, though, he sighed. "We need to pray about it, at the very least. A visit would be more than simply a handful of days, given the lengths she'll need to travel, but..." With another sigh, he gave Anca a tired smile. "I'll do my best to behave if she does join us."

Anca smiled at him and squeezed his hand as he took hers. She spent several hours praying to HaMelech about this potential visit, desperately wanting to be sure that this was not going to jeopardize anyone in Apple Ridge, before she drafted a letter for her sister.

Flick read it over, pointed out a handful of statements that the inquisitors would deem suspicious, and Anca returned to writing. Finally, when Flick said it proved no cause of concern for either Apple Ridge or them, Anca painstakingly folded it and delivered it to Rolandus.

He raised an eyebrow, looked at it, and then at Anca. "Flick knows?"

"He's already double checked for anything that would concern the inquisitors," Anca replied. She smiled slightly at Rolandus. "I know you're worried, but we've prayed over it and discussed it in depth."

The captain nodded slightly and carefully put the letter in the breast pocket of his jacket. "Alright, so long as everyone is on the same page. Last I remember, Flick said that he and your sister didn't get along well."

"They didn't... but I miss her, and I know Flick is happy to meet me where I'm at."

She watched as the patrol said their final goodbyes and left, leaving her to quietly return to her home and do some sewing.

Eventually, another letter returned; Adriata had accepted their invitation.

***

The next several weeks were spent in anxious preparation. Flick and Anca had purchased a new house while waiting for a reply, doing so simply for Drop and Shatter's sake. With the new home, there was a spare room that Anca could prepare for her sister. Drop and Shatter did what they could to help, too, especially when Anca could feel her head beginning to swim. Eventually, a coach pulled through Apple Ridge and stopped beside their home. Anca waited beside the door, leaning against the doorframe to keep from fainting as her children stood beside her. Flick looked out as well, and then approached to help Adriata from the carriage.

It was difficult to keep from grinning as Anca saw her sister, the familiar blue eyes and straight blonde hair of Adriata just as she remembered. Then, as Anca watched, Adriata turned and helped a smaller figure from the coach as well.

There was a child with her, a four-year-old curseborn girl with ruddy red skin and curly black hair that had been pulled into a haphazard braid.

Anca frowned slightly to herself.

Where was the child from? Adriata had never desired to have children before, much less as a Solari woman. Curseborns were said to be the result of bad karma, so the Solari church said. Adriata wouldn't have wanted to sully her name with taking a child of that appearance in. Anca's eyes softened as the little girl looked around, and she glanced at Drop and Shatter. "The two of you, why not see if she'd like to play?"

"She looks young, Mother," Drop said softly. "I don't know if she'll want to play with us."

Shatter nodded from beside his sister. "Her dress might get torn."

That was true; she was wearing a rather nice dress with frills and lace, something that Anca would feel horrid about getting ripped. Still, as Anca watched the girl's eyes flash to Drop and Shatter and then away, she shook her head. "Offer all the same. I can mend any tears, and I will happily do so."

She stood up from the doorframe, swayed before Shatter caught her hand, and then gave her stepson a bit of a smile. Adriata looked towards her and gave a restrained smile, and Anca gave a smile back. "It's so good to see you, Adriata!"

"I'll admit, I was surprised that you responded to my letter, but all the same, I'm glad we're here," Adriata replied. She looked down at the curseborn holding her hand. "Jean, my dear, this is your adoptive Aunt Anca."

Jean gave a crooked curtsy and Anca smiled lightly at her, though confusion continued to race through her head. When did Adriata decide to adopt a child? Why did she decide to adopt? Years ago, she had no desire to have children. Was this a ploy?

"It's wonderful to meet you, my dear. That is my husband, your uncle Flick, and these are my children, Drop and Shatter."

She watched as Jean's eyes flashed to the older children again and she gave a hint of a smile before it disappeared. Then, Anca looked at her children. Drop was the first to step forward, smiling though her dark eyes kept the guarded caution that she had inherited from Flick. "We were just going to go to the community garden and look for vegetables, did you want to come?"

Shatter nodded in agreement and then, crouching to be eye level with Jean, murmured something so quietly Anca couldn't hear. The girl's eyes lit up and she nodded rapidly before she looked at Adriata. "May I go?"

"Yes, but stay with them."

Anca smiled at her children as they ran off, Jean, in tow, before she looked at Adriata. Her sister hadn't moved much, though she did shift to watch her daughter go off to play, before she looked at Anca. Neither of them spoke for a while before Adriata murmured, "Your nose never did straighten out, did it?"

Subconsciously, Anca touched it and grimaced. "I suppose that's what happens when a High Inquisitor decides to break it, isn't it?"

"Indeed." Adriata watched her and Anca shifted. She knew this was a lead up into an argument; her sister always got a look on her face when she was about to scold her. Then, as Flick approached, Adriata said,

"I wish you had told me what was going on before it escalated. Who tricked you into following the Usurper?"

"I wasn't tricked," Anca said lightly, "and I'd rather not discuss this outside. I need to make dinner, and I am happy to continue our conversation while I do so."

Adriata followed her inside as Flick toted her things, and Anca settled at the table to begin making a loaf of bread. As she did, she glanced at Adriata. "Flick and I have made a good life here. He's gotten promoted to captain since we moved to Apple Ridge, and the children have grown quickly."

"I can see that."

Looking at her, Anca sighed. "Adriata, I hope you know that I was planning on telling you that Flick and I were married before everything happened. We wanted to invite you to dinner that night, and I was going to speak to you there, but then the ascention..." She trailed off, shook her head, and looked back at what she was doing. "I didn't mean for you to get caught up in any of the mess in Zanther."

"There was no way to keep me out of it, Anca, the moment High Inquisitor Alastar got involved. What sort of man did you marry to get the High Inquisitors after you? Is he safe for you to be around?" Adriata frowned, pulling her gloves off and setting them on the table. "You know I want what's best for you, but is he what's best?"

Anca rose an eyebrow. "You've waited six years to ask me this question, Adriata. What do you expect me to say?"

"The truth!"

"Fine! Flick denounced Solaris in the presence of the whole council, Adriata. I think he's more than safe, but returning to Zanther never will be. His father is still searching for us. Any group that comes from Zanther mentions that High Inquisitor Alastar is still searching for his son, a man who renounced Solaris and married a heretical witch." Adriata's eyes widened at Anca's words, making the younger of the two continue. "He's a vicious, cruel man who wants nothing but to kill us to save his dignity, Adriata. Flick Alastar is safe, Fernando Alastar is not."

Silence hung heavily over them, and Anca, after a moment, shook her head. "My husband is a safe man. He loves me fiercely, he loves our children. I will never question that." Adriata didn't speak, prompting Anca to murmur, "Enough of that. Who exactly is Jean? You said you never wanted children."

Her sister cleared her throat, composing herself after Anca's outburst. Part of Anca felt bad for the sudden sharpness in her tone, but she wasn't going to allow Adriata to speak poorly of Flick. They often argued, and she often allowed Adriata to have the final word, but she wasn't willing to do it now. As she decided this, her vision faded and she caught herself on the table edge.

"Anca? What's the matter?"

"I'll be fine, simply... faint," Anca murmured. She swallowed and hung her head. It took a moment as her vision left completely, and she felt her body go lax. From the foggy sound of Adriata quickly moving to her side, she was certain she terrified her sister. It wasn't until her vision returned and she felt that she could sit up did she speak again. "I... have fairly frequent fainting spells, is all. I worked myself up."

"That isn't normal."

"It is for me," Anca said softly. "It's been happening for a year and a half. My assumption is that I will need a chair to remain in soon enough, if it continues to grow worse." She met her sister's concerned blue eyes and smiled weakly.

Adriata frowned in return before she sighed. "If you're certain... What had you asked?"

"Jean."

"Ah, yes, my adopted daughter." Adriata settled in her seat once more, all the while watching Anca like a hawk. It was a reminder of what it was like in Zanther, the constant protective eyes on her whenever she was home. As Anca nodded, Adriata continued, "I adopted her last year; I was on a trip to Ashuran on business. It was the strangest thing, really. I hadn't at all meant to stop at an orphanage, but my coach broke down. It was such a horrid deluge that I had to take shelter. While I was there, she came straight to me. She sat in my lap and had me read to her. I left before they woke, but I just couldn't stop thinking about her. I turned back two days out and brought her home with me to Zanther. She's a good girl, really, but..."

Adriata trailed off for a moment and then shook her head. "Having a curseborn as your adoptive daughter is difficult." As she mused, she put a grape into her mouth. "People assume you've done something to deserve the bad karma, and doing her hair is an absolute mess with her horns."

Anca frowned at the words, propping her head on her hand. "You said you never wanted children; you went so far as to have a surgery to avoid conceiving."

"I still don't want children, but I wanted Jean," Adriata replied with a shrug. "Things change." She ate another grape and looked at Anca. "What about you? You've been married six years, haven't you and Flick decided a spawn of your own?"

Her chewing was loud in Anca's ears, and the younger of the two shifted. It was as though the room was too small now, especially as she inhaled to try and clear the air around her. Eventually, she shook her head. "No. I mean... we've tried but... it just... hasn't..." Her eyes began to sting and she wiped at them, staring at the ceiling in an attempt to keep from crying.

Adriata hummed softly. Anca couldn't tell if it was out of sympathy or thought, but it made her eyes prick further as her sister said, "I'm sorry, my dear. It really is a curse from Solaris—"

"I don't follow Solaris, Adriata. I haven't since meeting Marin at the infirmary," Anca interrupted. She wiped her eyes again. "I don't believe that Solaris has any power, and I don't believe that this is a curse. HaMelech is good and... and the inability to conceive has brought peace where I was once grieving the loss of pregnancy. It's a blessing, even if I didn't realize it at the time."

"Oh, I didn't mean anything by it, of course," Adriata said quickly. Her eyes shifted from aloof to the gentle, motherly look that Anca had grown accustomed to. "What I mean to say is that it's an absolute shame."

Anca wiped her eyes again, shaking her head. "I don't know, Adriata. I suppose it is, but... it's been so long. Seeing you with your daughter surprised me, especially when I was going... I was hoping..." She sighed and hung her head. "I'm sorry, I didn't mean to spoil the mood."

It took a moment before Adriata began to rub her shoulder, having abandoned her grapes on the table to focus solely on her sister. Anca leaned into the touch, sniffling softly. Flick came into the room after a moment, looked between the two, and murmured, "Should I go?"

"No," Anca said, shaking her head. "We're simply... catching up."

Her sister gave her a sad smile and Anca gave her a smile in return, wiped her eyes, and sighed. "We should call the children in. I hope Jean didn't tear her dress; I really don't mind mending any of it if she does, and I told my kids that."

Adriata nodded slightly and stood to get the children before Flick waved her off. "I'll do it. Knowing they're in the garden, they'll probably need some help bringing produce home... or keeping frogs there." He smiled at them, kissed Anca's forehead, and slipped out.

Anca watched him go and looked at Adriata. Her sister was staring after him, an unreadable expression on her face, before she looked at Anca. "He'd better be taking good care of you."

"He is."

The children were covered in mud when they returned, and Anca reassured Adriata that she'd tend to Jean's dress for her. Drop and

Shatter were beaming as their younger cousin held out a garden snail towards Anca, the little creature slowly moving about her hand. "She caught it herself."

"Very nicely done," Anca said, smiling at her niece as she inspected the snail. "You were very gentle. It's time for our friend to return to the outside, though."

Jean giggle, nodded, and raced after Shatter to return the snail to the bushes beside the door.

They played a game of charades after dinner, finding that Jean was an incredibly bright child while being so soft-spoken. It was only after the children had retired for bed, and Adriata bid Anca goodnight, that Anca looked at Flick. "She worries about me."

"I would assume so. Will you be alright with her staying with us for several months?"

"Yes... yes, I will."

Chapter Seven

Nearly Seven Years

Anca smiled slightly at Jean, watching as her niece quietly drew at the table. Drop was beside her, doing the same, though the drawings were vastly different; the four-year-old had decided to scribble some people while Drop, who was now twelve, did her best to draw the flowers sitting in front of her.

Shatter had gone to train with Flick, desiring nothing more than to become a Knight of the Long Road as soon as he was old enough.

"Don't you think Shatter is doing too much?" Drop asked suddenly, not looking up from her paper.

Sitting down, Anca tilted her head. "What do you mean, my darling fledgling?"

"If he's going to be a Knight of the Long Road, won't HaMelech call him?"

With a little hum, Anca settled in her seat. Jean was still drawing, but the curiosity in her eyes was betrayed briefly when she looked towards them. Finally, Anca said, "HaMelech might have called him, Drop, but we won't know unless he shares it with us. Sometimes, there's a passion that confirms what HaMelech desires for our lives."

"Hm... do you think HaMelech might call me to serve, too?"

"There's a good chance," Anca said with a nod. "It's not at all uncommon for young women to serve as Knights, if that's the path HaMelech has set before them. He could call you to be a dove healer, too, or simply to show charity within the town."

Drop hummed in thought. Jean kept her eyes on her paper before she lifted it and held it towards Anca. "Will Mama like it?"

"She'll love it," Anca replied. She smiled fondly at her niece, studying the scrawling on her page before she ruffled her hair. "You're such a wonderful artist, my dear."

Jean beamed and returned to her work.

Anca glanced towards the room where Adriata and Jean had been resting. Her sister tended to sleep in later than the child did, often slipping from their quarters closer to lunch. To be fair, she also remained awake until the wee morning hours. Anca knew it was due to the work schedule that Adriata adopted while in Zanther; being the mistress of a brothel did that.

Adriata had first taken the job up to provide for them while they were young. With their parents having died no more than eight years after Anca's birth, leaving Adriata twelve and angry, there were no other choices. Adriata refused to let them enter an orphanage, claiming that it was against Solaris's will, nor did she wish to write to any adults they knew at the time. They were Cassys, after all, which meant they could do it on their own.

A sad smile flickered over Anca's face at the memories, and she closed her eyes.

Things had settled out after that. It had been ten years of scraping together what they had. Adriata did well in the red-light district, and eventually she became a madame. Anca was proud of her sister for making her way in the world, but she wished things had happened differently.

Jean climbed into Anca's lap, startling her. "Yes, my love?"

"Did you live with Mama before?"

Of course it was a question like that. Anca chuckled and nodded, wrapping her shawl around the little girl and her own shoulders. "I did, yes."

"Did you like living with her?"

"Yes."

Jean hummed and cuddled into her side, kicking her legs as she thought. Then, she said, "I like being here."

Anca smiled, pulled her tighter, and swayed. "I'm glad you do. I like having you and your mama here. It's wonderful having you."

"I like having you here, too," Drop said. Jean beamed between them and settled against Anca.

They remained at the table for a little while before Adriata joined them, her hair messy and the bags under her eyes pronounced. She yawned, waved slightly at them, and settled at the table. "Good morning."

"Good afternoon," Anca corrected gently. "It's nearly noon."

Adriata hummed at her to show that she heard before she propped her head on the table. "Jean, what have you been up to since waking up?"

"Playing with Drop and Aunt Anca."

"Ah, hopefully you weren't bothering your adoptive aunt."

Jean shook her head and hopped down from Anca's lap. She quietly handed Adriata her drawing, got a smile and a pat on her head, before she bounced to Drop and tugged on her hand. "Can we go look for frogs? Please?"

"I believe there are nettle mice around the corner if the two of you would like to find them," Anca said. "Just be careful when it comes to their fur. I don't want to be picking spines from your hands the rest of the afternoon."

Both of the girls ran out and Anca glanced at Adriata. "You're certain you want her to be calling me her adoptive aunt? It doesn't feel right, having her call me that. She's my niece even if we don't share blood."

"You know what the tenets say," Adriata said. She stretched and shook her head. "If you don't differentiate blood from not, then Solaris—"

"Adriata, I'm not going to follow Solaris again."

The two locked eyes and Adriata frowned. "You haven't even considered it?"

"Not in the slightest," Anca murmured. "I'm happy following HaMelech. It can be hard, I have to work at it, and there are times where I don't know what's happening, but I know He loves me. He brought Flick into my life, my friends... He kept you and I safe in Zanther." She smiled at her sister, her voice growing softer. "I know He loves you, too."

Adriata looked away from her. She stood, crossed to the hearth to put on the kettle for tea, and stood watching the flames. Finally, she murmured, "You know that High Inquisitor Alastar is still looking for you, correct?" Anca swallowed as her sister tightened her robe over her shoulders, her gaze never once leaving the fire. "The inquisitors personally delivered your letter to me. They're certain you're still with Flick, and they're certain that they will capture and execute him for high treason."

"Adriata—"

"So long as you remain in the nation of Dusnar, and do not show your face in Zanther, let alone Yegreydal, you'll be safe, Anca... but I won't be able to protect you forever. Not from them, not from Solaris, not from your foolish dreams."

Her sister refused to look at her still and Anca, slowly, crossed to her. She could feel her vision was hazy the moment she stood, but she crossed to the fire all the same and caught Adriata's hand. Then, as her legs gave out, she sank to the ground. "Is this why you took so long to write?"

"Among other reasons, Anca." Adriata looked down at her then, her face stoic. She held Anca's hand tightly before she sighed and shook her head. "This visit won't be able to take as long as I'd like, as they're still watching my home. It's a breath of fresh air to get out of the city walls, and allow Jean to see the world, but it's most certainly a dangerous one all the same."

"Why didn't you tell me when you arrived?"

"And risk you turning me away?" Adriata laughed. She crouched before Anca and stroked some hair from her face. "I know what your husband thinks of me, dear sister. I'm not stupid."

Anca frowned. Flick didn't care for her sister, that was true, but he wouldn't have forced Adriata out... would he? She sighed and shook her head. "We wouldn't have."

"Hm... I don't know if I believe you, Anca." Adriata kissed her forehead. "Now, time for you to get up and sit. You're lucky you didn't fall into the fire. You and Flick need to discuss what you can do for the fainting spells. I'm inclined to believe that you should remain sitting as much as possible. Whatever condition this is could very well grow worse, could it not?"

With trembling hands, Anca slowly stood upright. She swayed, holding tighter to her sister, before she crossed to her chair and sat in it once more.

HaMelech had her. His strength was made perfect in her weakness. He was keeping her from harm, He was good.

Sucking in a breath, the woman nodded faintly at her sister's suggestion. "We've discussed it. I've been the one worried about what implications it might bring."

"Implications?" Adriata repeated, her eyebrow raised. She settled into her chair as well, her blue eyes never leaving Anca. "What implications, and who would assume them?" Anca looked towards her, watching as her gaze flashed between annoyed, reserved disgust, and finally the cool apathy she tried desperately to maintain.

Anca wondered if she was assuming that Flick would look down at her for using a wheeled chair to move around, though that wasn't who Anca worried about. In fact, Flick had been the last one to suggest using a wheeled chair to allow for Anca to return to working or otherwise rejoin life as she missed.

Anca shook her head. "It wouldn't be Flick that I'd worry about," she said softly. "It's others here at Apple Ridge. We've been struggling to conceive since we were wed, and people are currently whispering about that. My concern is that they'll have more to whisper about should I find myself bound—"

"I wouldn't use the term bound, Anca, nor would I worry about them," Adriata replied. The kettle had begun to boil, prompting her to cross to the fire once more and pour two mugs of hot water over tea leaves. "A wheeled chair will give you more freedom than you currently have, my dear, and that would allow you to deal with the naysayers yourself. As for them, I wouldn't worry myself over them. People will talk, as you and I both know. They'll continue to speak of it, over and over, regardless as to what else they could converse about. You simply happen to be the largest of targets as you and your husband give the biggest reaction."

"That's easy for you to say, Adriata. You don't have people whispering about your inability—"

"I have Solari worshippers whispering about my karma due to my adopting of Jean," Adriata interrupted again. She set the mugs down in front of Anca, glanced at the window, and lowered her voice. "I may not know what it's like to have people muttering behind my back about my bedroom habits, but I know very well that people do comment about my adopted daughter, and me, and often question how I may become anything even while working in a Temple."

Swallowing, Anca nodded slightly. It had been callous of her to assume that Adriata didn't know what it was like, even more so as Adriata glanced at the window a second time to see if the girls had returned. Adriata was likely doing all she could to keep Jean safe despite rumors and coldhearted remarks, just as Anca was doing her best to keep her children from being involved in her problems.

The shorter of the two exhaled and nodded again. "You're right... I'm sorry."

Adriata hummed in return, and Anca stared at her mug. Neither of them spoke again until Flick and Shatter arrived home for lunch. Shatter was covered in mud and a grin. "Mother! Mother, I disarmed Uncle Rolandus!"

"You did?" Anca glanced at Flick, received a bit of a smile and nod, and then looked at Shatter. "All by yourself? That's incredible, my little raven!"

She embraced Shatter, who held tightly to her. As she pet his hair, Anca couldn't help but inhale and close her eyes to savor his hug. He was growing too quickly. They both were. He was disarming captains today, tomorrow he would be receiving his own mantle. She wasn't ready for it, neither was she ready for Drop to become a grown woman in the next several years. Anca tightened her grip slightly before she pulled away from her stepson, searched his face, and kissed his forehead. "I'm so proud of you."

Shatter beamed, dashed to the counter to grab a crust of bread, and backpedaled to the door. "I'm going to go tell Jean and Drop!"

"They're out by the garden, collecting slugs, last I heard," Anca said.

Adriata waved slightly to the boy as he raced out, and then she looked at Flick. Anca followed her gaze, a tired smile flickering over her face as she watched him carefully prop his quarterstaff against the door and then pull off his muddy boots.

He glanced at them and smiled. "Rolandus gave him a bit of an early go, but for an eleven-year-old, we're really quite pleased with his progress," he said. Straightening up, he tousled his hair to fix it and then gave Anca a kiss. "He's got the good makings of a knight about him."

"Good." Anca returned his kiss and fixed a strand of his hair falling over his eyes. "Drop was commenting on the time he was spending with you."

"I'm sure she was. I've yet to say anything to her, but Olare, Rolandus, and I have the feeling that she'll be joining us soon enough," Flick said. He sat beside her, smiled, and then began to clean his knife.

Anca nodded to herself. That made sense; she had a feeling, too, that Drop wouldn't be a dove healer. Still, it was not their place to tell her what HaMelech willed until He desired them to do so. As she thought, she caught sight of Adriata shifting in her seat.

"The two of you need to discuss accommodations for Anca," she finally said.

Flick looked at her, and then Anca. "Did you have another fainting spell?"

"It wasn't bad, and Adriata was there to catch me," Anca said.

Adriata frowned. "She fell beside the fire while we were speaking."

"Why were you beside the fire? The bread had finished earlier today, my love." Flick's worried eyes flashed to her again. "If you had fallen in, I would never forgive myself for being elsewhere—"

"I'm fine, Flick," Anca reassured. She took his hand, his knife long forgotten as he clung to her.

In just a handful of moments, Anca could see the same young man she married nearly seven years ago. His eyes had clouded over with the same fear that reflected at her when they had been found out, and, as she held his hand, she could feel his pulse rapidly beating beneath her fingers. Anca reached out and stroked his cheek with one hand, pressing her forehead to his own. "My love, I'm alright."

"You really aren't, Anca," Flick whispered. "We don't know what's wrong and it angers me. I pray to HaMelech that maybe, just maybe, He'll reveal what's going on." He sighed and shook his head. "I hate seeing you in this state. You've not been able to work, and I know how much you loved tending to patients, and you're unable to be in the garden like you used to. It makes me ache, knowing that you've lost a part of yourself being ill."

Anca looked down.

He was right, but she didn't want to admit it. It was a matter of pride, as much as she hated admitting that more, as well as the desire to be anything but a disappointment to him. Slowly, Anca exhaled, and whispered, "I don't want to use a wheeled chair if I can avoid it."

"Why?"

Slowly, she shook her head.

"She's afraid of the nasty comments she'll hear after dealing with them this long," Adriata said. Anca glared towards her and she shrugged. "I can imagine that part of it is the desire to keep from looking weak, on top of not wanting to feel broken."

"But... you aren't broken, Anca," Flick said softly. He squeezed her hand and Anca looked at him again. "HaMelech didn't make you broken, your body simply works differently than others. That doesn't make you broken."

"I can't carry a child, Flick, I'd constitute that as broken."

Her husband frowned, sighed, and shook his head. "I don't agree, but I also know I can't argue and win." He kissed her forehead. "I would much rather you use a wheeled chair and deal with any scorn that comes your way than witness you die to yourself in a way that HaMelech didn't call you to. He never once asked you to stop living, did He? Or to stop tending to His creations?" Anca shook her head slightly, and Flick made a triumphant little sound. "Then it's settled. I can commission a chair to be made for you, and you can do things you enjoy again. It'll be different, I know it will, but anything I can do to see you smile again, or laugh outside without fear of fainting, I'll do."

"Are you sure?"

He nodded again and Adriata, from across the table, crossed one leg over the other. "As much as I hate to agree with him, simply on the grounds that I dislike him for trying to find you in a brothel when we first met, I can at least say that he has your best interests in mind."

A terse laugh answered her, and Flick stood. "I'll go speak to a tradesman now, the same one who made Olare's arm, if I can find him." Flick kissed her head and looked at Adriata. "I did apologize for that, by the way."

"Still doesn't mean I forgive you for assuming Anca was a prostitute."

Anca rolled her eyes at the bickering before Flick hurried out, leaving her with her sister again. "I suppose we should call the children in?"

Adriata nodded just as Shatter raced inside, panting. "Mother, I can't find Drop and Jean."

"What?"

Shatter shook his head as Anca stood, swayed, and caught herself on the table. "I can't find them. I looked in the garden, I checked the field, and I went to our favorite climbing tree. I can't find them."

Adriata bolted upright as soon as Shatter said this, tied her robe tighter around herself, and rushed to the door. "Anca, you stay here in case they return."

"I should help—"

"Absolutely not! You'll work yourself into a faint if you do," Adriata said sternly. She didn't leave any room for Anca to argue before she was gone, Shatter following quickly after.

Anca stared after her sister, a pit growing in her stomach.

Where did the girls go? They had just been by the house, hadn't they? She remembered hearing them laughing before Flick and Shatter returned home, and that hadn't been long before. Flick hadn't taken them, otherwise he would have said something.

Without anything else that she could do, Anca held her hands up and began to pray.

"HaMelech, You know where the girls are. You know where my daughter is, You know where my niece went. Please, Father, let them be safe. Keep them from harm, let it be only that they wandered off and neglected to tell us. Let someone find them and return them to me, let the town discover them unharmed."

As she prayed, she heard the town's bell begin to toll, signaling that there was trouble. Shatter must have reached a captain of the knights, who had sounded the alarm. Soon, everyone would be looking for the missing children. Anca squeezed her eyes shut tighter. "Please keep them safe, Lord, regardless of where they are. Let us find them swiftly, unscathed..." She trailed off, her voice catching. He knew her heart, and He knew a part of her desired them safely back to avoid the whispers, too. "Forgive me," she whispered. "My worries should be on the girls only, not my perception... please, forgive me, cleanse my heart of my selfishness."

A strange sort of peace settled over her as she sat there, praying fervently, before little footsteps hurried into the room. Anca lifted her head to find Drop and Jean before her, straw and mud in their hair and their little bodies breathless. "There you are!" She enveloped them into a tight hug, clinging to them. "Where on torus did you go? We were looking for you, they rang the bells as you were missing!"

She pulled away as Drop scratched her arm, looking down. Jean held tightly to her hand, and finally, as Anca searched their faces, Drop mumbled, "I brought Jean to meet the sheepdogs. Uncle Rolandus didn't mind me going the other day, and I thought Jean would like to see them. We heard the bells and came back because we didn't know what was happening."

"You... oh, Drop, why hadn't you thought about what would happen if you simply ended up missing? My love, we thought something happened to you!" Tears streaked down Drop's face, and Anca pulled them to herself again. Though she couldn't see Jean's tears, she could feel the little curseborn shaking in her arms. "We were terrified..."

"I'm sorry," Jean whispered. Drop nodded, and Anca stroked through their hair. It did nothing to scold them further, especially as she realized how frightened they were once they had heard the bells. Anca sighed softly and closed her eyes.

"Thank HaMelech you're safe," she whispered. "Thank HaMelech that it was simply the two of you wandering off without telling anyone, and nothing serious..."

The girls continued to hold tightly to her, eventually only pulling away when Anca kissed their foreheads and then slowly stood. "I need to let them know that you've been found," she said.

"I can do it—"

"No, you will not, Drop," Anca said sternly. She stopped, hung her head, and then looked at her stepdaughter.

Her dark eyes were wide, filled with tears again. Anca shook her head. "My love, I can't let you leave the house right now, not when the whole town is searching for you. I need both you and Jean to stay inside; then you won't wander off and get lost again. Do you understand?"

Drop nodded, though Anca knew that her stepdaughter didn't like it. Rather than continuing to argue, she slowly made her way to the door and looked out. A handful of people were passing by their home, calling Drop and Jean's names, and Anca waved them down.

"We still haven't found them," one said, wiping his brow. "I'm sorry, Anca, but—"

"They're returned home; they heard the bells and ran here as quickly as they could," Anca interrupted softly. "Thank you for looking, can you please spread the word that they've been found?"

She watched them go before she returned to the home. There, they waited silently until Flick and Adriata, with Shatter in tow, returned. Anca didn't remain in the room as Adriata scolded Jean for disappearing, nor did she want to listen to Flick speak to Drop about responsibility. Instead, she laid down on the bed and stared at the ceiling, thanking HaMelech that the girls had made it home safely.

Chapter Eight

Seven and a Quarter Years, Part 1

Anca held tighter to Adriata as they hugged, closing her eyes to keep from crying. "I hope we can see you again soon," she whispered.

Adriata petted her hair, holding her just as tightly. It brought a sense of familiarity to Anca, leaning into her sister's touch as she was silently consoled. "I'm sure you will, Anca. My hope is that our meetings can eventually be more frequent, though it'll be difficult with the current council in Zanther."

She pulled away and Anca sank into her wheeled chair, fixing her tear-filled gaze on Jean. Her niece had celebrated a birthday while with them, freshly five and full of questions. She had grown several inches taller, too, as she played with Drop and Shatter through the summer and had developed a keen sense of understanding.

Drop had grown too, growing ever closer to a young woman now that she was thirteen. Drop was far more concerned about keeping her cousin out of trouble, too. Rolandus had commented that her responsibility had become far better after the scare, and he lightly suggested to Anca and Flick that she join him with the sheepdogs if she wanted to. That meant that Jean went with them, and many hours were spent listening to the girls talk about the dogs and the care they were giving them.

Jean shifted, scratching the back of her leg with her foot quietly before she looked at Anca. "I'll miss you. Can you come visit?"

"I wish I could, my love, but Zanther isn't safe for us to go to," Anca murmured. "You are always welcome to come and see us, though. Any time you want to come, you're more than welcome." She hugged Jean tightly, closed her eyes, and inhaled deeply. She was going to miss the little curseborn more than she wanted to admit.

Flick rested his hand on her shoulder after she pulled away, his eyes gentle when she met them. He gave her a sad smile before he ruffled Jean's hair. "Thanks for spending time with us, kiddo."

"Bye, Adopted Uncle Flick." Jean hugged him and he sighed, holding her for a moment.

Even during their stay, Adriata insisted that Jean maintain proper reference to her adopted family.

Anca watched as Flick's shoulders stiffened before he tightened his hug. Neither of them liked it, but Jean didn't listen. She obeyed her mother, which was good, but it did break Anca's heart. She watched as her sister and niece piled into the carriage and looked out, waving as the vehicle lurched forward on six spindly legs, before they were gone.

After watching them go, Anca wheeled herself back inside. Marin was kind enough to have given her the day off to say goodbye to her family, and, while Anca was certain she didn't entirely know what it was like, her friend knew enough to console her.

"Are you going to work?" Flick asked softly, following her inside.

The children had run off to play as soon as the carriage was gone, leaving Anca and Flick alone with their thoughts. Anca shook her head slightly. "I don't know. I may, if only to soothe my heart."

"You miss them already, don't you?"

Anca nodded slightly before she sighed. "I miss the idea of what could have happened if we weren't run out of Zanther, my love. I desperately want to see them more than just their visit, but..." Trailing off, Anca looked at the ceiling. She felt her husband's hand find her own, holding it tightly, before she whispered, "I didn't dare say it while Adriata was here, but I'm angry at her for showing up with Jean. I love Jean dearly, please don't misunderstand but... but she told me years ago that she refused to have children. Then, suddenly, she appears with a child that... that..."

"That made you ache, knowing that we want another of our own?" Flick finished.

Slowly, Anca nodded. She turned to face Flick, her voice growing softer. "I'm afraid that Marin will tell me that carrying a child, if we conceive, will kill me. I mean... look at me. I can't stand without support most days, and I'm in this chair."

"And you're beautiful and a fighter," Flick said. He kissed her gently, searching her face. Anca felt more seen by him as he did so, his hand cupping her cheek gently. "Anca, you're perhaps the strongest woman I know. You've gone through seven years of mourning, almost three years of the fainting spells. There's no way I could argue that you aren't strong."

She offered a little smile at his words before she sighed.

If she was strong, she needed to lean further into HaMelech. Her heart ached, and she knew that, when it did, she tried desperately to pull from HaMelech. It was the nature of the flesh, desiring nothing but a removal from everyone and everything in an attempt to keep from being hurt. With everything that was going on, Anca knew heavily that she was going to continue this path if she didn't trust Him as she was called to do.

With this in mind, she held slightly tighter to Flick's hand and closed her eyes. "I need you to pray over me, please." Flick made a soft sound of acknowledgement, but remained silent. Anca sighed and continued. "I... I can sense that I'm trying desperately to pull away from everything good in life, Flick. I'm hurt, I'm confused and... I hate to say this, but I'm worried that HaMelech has forgotten me. I know in the Holy Texts that He is faithful, and He always lavishes His children with blessings but... right now, I have all but forgotten the blessings we have. Please, as my husband and the head of our household, I need you to pray over me, more than ever."

"I hope you know that I've always covered you in my prayers," Flick whispered. "Each night, I do so, but I am more than honored and privileged to pray over you right now."

Anca nodded slightly at him as he took both of her hands. His forehead rested against her own, a touch that felt comforting yet hollow, and she exhaled as he whispered, "HaMelech... help us. Hear our cries, take our hurts. We thank You for being the loving God You are, and we are in awe of Your gentleness towards us. Great Creator, we lean into You now. We rest in Your arms, as we are too weary to stand on our own feet. You're so kind, You're so loving and You desire nothing more than to hold our hearts in Your hands with the care of a father. Thank you for being faithful and trustworthy.

"As we sit before you, kneeling before Your throne, I lift Anca to You. She's exhausted, HaMelech, and her spirit is weary. It has been seven years of battle, of grief, and of heartbreak. Even the blessings we've experienced have faded into the shadows that creep around us, and we desire nothing more than to have Your comforting presence over us. The visit with Adriata and Jean was hard, but we thank You even for the difficulties that it brought. We were able to be family again, a family that was together despite our differences."

As he prayed, Anca did her best not to cry. Hearing his gentle phrasing of what was going on made it feel more real, realer than she wanted to admit. Then, amid his prayers, two smaller hands rested on her shoulders. She spared a single glance back to see Shatter was standing there, respectfully bowing his head as Flick continued to pray. Out of the corner of her eye, she caught sight of Drop behind Flick. She truly never wanted the children to be involved. This wasn't their battle to worry about, nor was it their burden to carry.

As the children, from time to time, murmured agreements to Flick's words, however, a sense of peace washed over her.

Whether it was her own mind attempting to convince her that this was alright, or it truly was HaMelech putting her at ease, Anca wasn't entirely sure. What she did know, though, was that her heart swelled with pride as she heard Shatter's soft voice.

"Thank you, HaMelech, for Mother. Thank you for her kindness towards Drop and I, thank you for making her our mother. Thank you for all that You have given us through her, and thank you for showing us what a woman following You looks like."

As her family surrounded her with their prayers, Anca closed her eyes again and simply breathed.

***

The next several weeks were filled with a whirlwind of work.

She returned to working at the Temple, this time handling incoming patients and paperwork from the safety of a desk and her wheeled chair rather than going from room to room to complete documents. Marin and the other doves were certain to visit her each day, oftentimes commenting how thankful they were for her return and her clerical skills. Anca found that she really did enjoy working at the entrance of the Temple; while it wasn't as intimate as doing housecalls, the influx of people who spoke to her made her feel more included than she had been for a while.

There were, of course, questions about her absence. She knew there were whispers circulating the town about her, but each time she heard them, she tried a different tactic; she prayed to HaMelech that whoever started it, and those who were continuing the rumors, might have a change of heart.

Many individuals wanted to know about the wheeled chair. Often, it resulted in a comment about how smart the idea was or, otherwise, that she was blessed to have a husband who was able to get one made for her. With the chair, too, she was able to return to the garden and tend to the plants she had tenderly planted years before.

Drop and Shatter both attended Knight of the Long Road training. Dinners with Olare, Rolandus, and Marin brought discussion of the children's talents and callings after they ate, all the while pointing towards both of them joining the Knights if they wanted to. Anca could tell that Flick was nearly bursting with pride as Olare informed him of Shatter's progress with the sword, his smile nearly contagious as he glanced at her. "We could have two Knights, my love."

"If they desire to join the call," Anca reminded gently. She couldn't help but smile herself, thinking about the children. "You'll want to speak to them once they wake. You must remember that it's their walk with HaMelech, dear, not ours."

"I know, I know. I'm just thrilled to know they're doing so well."

"They're doing wonderfully," Rolandus said amid a sip of his tea. "Drop has the makings of a fine scout, even for a handful of weeks joining me. I'm proud of them."

Anca smiled at the words, drinking her tea quietly as well, before Olare cleared his throat. "Moving to a different topic... Flick, we received word that inquisitors were sighted closer to Apple Ridge than ever. They've yet to make it towards these walls, but Rolandus and I, as well as the other captains, are getting concerned that they may be looking for you here."

The smile faded from Anca's lips at the news, and she looked at Flick. Adriata might have been followed, or they assumed Flick was wherever she was visiting. "You don't think they will come here, do you?"

"Perhaps," Olare said softly. "I don't know what they're doing, but I haven't seen inquisitors without a patrol of guards before."

Flick frowned, lost in thought as he tapped the table with one hand. Anca studied her husband, finding nothing but interest on his face. She desperately wished he would show some sort of concern about this, but as he remained silent, she simply waited. Finally, he shook his head. "The man who sired me is smart, but he is also prideful; he will not admit that I'm a cote if he is so against my sharing of his bloodline. He will not inform the inquisitors that I'm a cote as well. Doing so will force him to confront the fact that I'm related to him and share that ability." He looked around the table, his eyes lingering on Anca briefly. "They will be looking for me in this form, not my mantle. If they enter Apple Ridge, we will show them hospitality, but we will not be unprepared."

"Flick, what if he told them of the children? They haven't received their mantles yet," Anca murmured. She found Marin's hand and gripped it, exchanging a worried look at her friend. "They'll know what Marin looks like, and myself."

"And it's been seven years. If it's one thing I remember about my father, it's how distant his memory can be when he wishes to forget." Flick offered a sad smile. "My love, this isn't ideal, but HaMelech is on our side. I stand by my decision. Should they enter Apple Ridge, we will allow them to search while I hide my true nature. I'm sure they've got a writ from the High Council allowing an arrest in the nation of Dusnar."

Slowly, Anca nodded. She wasn't sure if this would be the best option, but as her husband stood resolved, she didn't argue. Instead, she glanced at Marin, and then at Olare and Rolandus. Each of them nodded in return before they bowed their heads and prayed. Most of the prayer was about courage, and discernment, about the coming weeks.

Anca was distracted even as Marin spoke beside her, her fingers trembling slightly with the potential of the inquisitors finding them. HaMelech was good, though, and would keep them safe.

Once their friends left, Anca looked at Flick. He had deflated, his shoulders sagged and his head in his hands. Anca's eyes softened and she slowly moved her chair to sit beside him. Then, as softly as she could, she murmured, "You're worried they'll know, aren't you?"

"I already forced you and the children through torture once," he said back, not looking at her. "I hate the idea of making you go through it again."

Anca pulled him near and began to stroke his hair. He sighed and relaxed in her arms, but she knew he was still transfixed on solving the issue of inquisitors. Finally, she murmured, "HaMelech will protect us, as you said. He has a plan, and I know that His plan is good." Flick nodded against her chest and Anca kissed his head. "Should we tell the children?"

"I'm not sure," he sighed. He pulled away and rubbed his forehead. "I don't want them caught off guard, but I also want to avoid panicking them. The inquisitors will be looking for me, rather than them. I'm a traitor to the nation, remember?"

Giving him a wry smile, Anca shook her head. "And we're affiliated with you. I'm sure there's nothing more that that man would like than to make you suffer, slowly and painfully, and using us is the best way to do that."

"All the more reason I'm worried about them coming to look for us," he said. He stood and began to pace, running a hand through his hair, before he looked at Anca. "Whatever happens, my desire is to be obedient to HaMelech. I pray that obedience, at this time, is simply remaining quiet and moving forward with our faith."

They fell into a fitful sleep, and Anca awoke the next morning to tend to the children and send Flick to the stables to work with the recruits. She had settled down for tea when there was a knock at the door, rather firm and decisive. With a frown, she wheeled to the entrance and opened the door only to freeze.

When Rolandus and Olare had spoken of inquisitors being close, they had never mentioned the potential of arrival overnight. Now, as Anca stared up at two figures in white pearlescent armor and shadowed faces, she felt her heart leap to her throat and bile follow just as quickly.

Shaking it off, however, she managed, "Good morning. What can I do for you?"

One of the inquisitors shifted slightly, his stance moving from poised to looking towards her. Anca could feel her heart pounding in her ears, especially as the man said, "Good morning, ma'am. We're inquisitors sent from the city of Blackrock to identify and retrieve a fugitive under the written orders of the Council on behalf of Zanther's High Inquisitor Alastar. Are you the only occupant of the home, and is there anyone else here with you?"

Was she? No, Drop was with her. Praise HaMelech that Flick and Shatter were out; they had time to prepare for the inquisitors searching for them. Slowly, Anca shook her head. "No, my daughter is here as well. My husband and son are currently training."

"May we see your daughter? Routine inspection as we search for our quarry."

Anca nodded faintly and turned her chair towards the home. "My love, please come here."

"Yes, Mother?" Drop rounded the corner and froze, her eyes wide. The inquisitors looked toward her and the one who spoke before, whom Anca assumed was relatively new to the position, chuckled softly.

"You needn't be afraid, child. You aren't who we're looking for."

Anca found her daughter beside her and held her hand to reassure her, her voice growing as steady as she could manage as she asked, "Who are you looking for?"

The younger of the two glanced at his companion, who shook his head slightly. "That isn't a concern," the second said gruffly. "It is a Solari matter, not for a Kingsman to worry about."

Anca bit her tongue and nodded all the same. Then, as she watched the two murmur to each other, she swallowed. They likely just arrived and had nowhere to rest for the evening, or their stay. As much as she disliked inquisitors, she knew that hospitality wasn't to be offered everywhere should the remainder of the town find out.

With this in mind, she cleared her throat just as they turned away. "Sirs?" They looked toward her, and she swallowed again. "You must have just arrived in Apple Ridge. Do you have any place you're staying while here?"

Both inquisitors recoiled, and Drop's grip on her hand tightened, as Anca looked at them. She was just as surprised as they were, given what they were here to do, but the little voice in the back of her mind that whispered this was the right thing to do spoke volumes louder than her terror. After following HaMelech as long as she did, she knew that this was his Breath speaking, and obeying this prompting was required of her. Flick would understand if she explained that to him, though she wasn't entirely sure if he would be incredibly pleased regardless.

Either way, she shifted in her seat. "I don't mean to be so bold in asking but... we do not receive many inquisitors in Apple Ridge, and given that most, if not all, of the inhabitants of this town are not fans of Solari police..." she trailed off, swallowed, and shook her head. "I'm not sure if you will find any places to stay while here."

They looked at each other again before the older one nodded. "Might as well take the offer. It'd be a warm bed and home-cooked meals rather than a tent and whatever we can hunt," he said.

"If I may, as I have not confirmed with my husband, I will send word to him immediately to be certain that he allows this as well," Anca said. She looked at Drop, who nodded slightly, and hurried inside to get a parchment and quill. As soon as she received it, Anca penned a quick message to Flick, warning him of the inquisitors and informing him that she would like to extend room and board to the two. Then, she carefully folded it and handed it to Drop. "Kindly run this to your father, and simply bring me word of his approval or denial," she said, staring at the girl.

She could see flashes of fear in Drop's eyes, likely memories of the last time they saw any inquisitors. Anca's nose ached at the reminder, too, but she forced that from her mind as the inquisitors stepped aside for the young lady to race off.

Then, once they were alone, Anca gestured inside. "I was settling to drink some tea, if you would like to join. At the very least, please wait until my daughter brings news as to your stay."

It took a moment before they agreed, and soon Anca found herself sitting across from the inquisitors as she sipped at her drink. In an effort to fill the silence, she murmured, "Surely the council in Blackrock sent you with more than just instructions to find someone?"

"They did," the younger of the two said. His companion looked at him, and he shrugged. Clearly, he didn't think Anca was a threat to their mission, especially as he said, "We've a description, and a first name. I don't suppose you've heard of a man named 'Flick' here, have you?"

Anca cursed herself silently and sipped her tea.

She hated to lie, as that was a sin. She closed her eyes for a moment before she gave a bit of a nod.

"Can you point him out to us?"

Anca slowly nodded again just as Drop hurried into the room. "Mother?"

All eyes turned to look at her, and she shifted. "Papa said he'd be honored to host them during their stay."

"Oh, good," Anca murmured. She looked to the inquisitors, who had stood. As they did, she felt her heart sink to her toes. The younger of the two glanced at her.

"I... hm, I thought we were going to ask you something but I don't seem to recall. We'll return closer to sundown for the evening, thank you for your hospitality Mrs..."

How had they forgotten what they were speaking about? Anca looked at Drop, whose face had gone three shades paler than normal. Her daughter knew that lying was wrong, too, and so she sighed. "Mrs. Alastar."

"Ah, Mrs. Alastar. Excellent, thank you. We'll inquire for directions back should we need them."

With that, they left.

Anca glanced at Drop. She could see her confusion was just as evident on her daughter's face as her own. "Did... they just walk out?"

"They did... Mother, you told them we are Alastars."

"I also had said I could point out your father... and... they forgot." She looked at Drop, releasing a breath, before she pulled her into a tight hug. “I’m so proud of your bravery speaking with them.”

"I’m terrified," Drop whispered. She held tighter to Anca, and the older woman stroked her inky black hair gently, kissing her Temple, as Drop breathed, "Mother, I remember… I remember all of what happened and…"

"And HaMelech has a plan for this, my little raven," Anca whispered back. "We'll be safe. I trust it."

Chapter Nine

Seven and a Quarter Years, Part 2

Anca sat fidgeting until Flick slipped into their bedroom. He ran a hand through his hair, looked at her, and shook his head. "I really hoped you hadn't heard from the Breath of HaMelech in inviting them to stay with us."

"Believe me, I wouldn't have offered otherwise," Anca replied. She shifted. "They asked if I knew of any 'Flicks' here, and if I could point you out."

"Did you say 'yes'?"

"I couldn't lie, Flick. HaMelech is very clear—"

"Anca, I'm terrified of what may come of that, but I'm proud of you for not sinning." Flick gave a tiny smile and continued to pace. "Though... you didn't come by the stables while I was there. Why didn't they have you show them where I was?"

She stared up at him, unsure of her answer. She shook her head, offered a weak laugh, and then whispered, "I don't know. They just...

forgot. I don't know if they simply don't remember, or if HaMelech is doing something, but it frightens me."

"I'll give the glory to HaMelech, regardless of what really happened," Flick said. He pulled his feathered shawl over his shoulders and inhaled. "I suppose they'll be here soon enough for dinner."

"I suppose."

Anca watched as he shifted, preparing to melt with the mantle, before he frowned. He smoothed the feathers out, took a deep breath, and then cursed. In the same breath, he muttered a brief prayer of repentance, and looked at Anca. "I'm not shifting."

"What do you mean?"

"My mantle isn't working. I can't take my cote form."

She blinked at him.

That was bad. That meant he couldn't hide his appearance. Anca inhaled, her vision beginning to grow hazy. Why had HaMelech allowed it to happen? Was He trying to teach them something, or was Flick meant to be captured? She sucked in another breath, feeling her body beginning to fold in on itself, before Flick held her upright. "Anca, are you alright?"

"Hm..."

Her head rested on Flick's shoulder as he stroked her hair, holding her until she returned fully to her senses and slowly sat up. "Was... it a long one?"

"Not terribly. You must be incredibly stressed."

Anca nodded faintly before there was a knock on the door.

"I'll get it," Flick murmured. "Wish me luck, my dear."

Anca followed him slowly, watching as he opened the door to reveal the two inquisitors. She couldn't quite hear them talking, but Flick eventually stepped aside to let them in. "Will you be removing your armor to eat with us?" he asked, glancing at Anca with a weak smile.

The inquisitors looked between one another before the older shrugged. "We won't be returning to Apple Ridge should we fail to find our target," he said. "Honestly, it's against protocol to give appearances or names if we aren't with other inquisitors, but, given you're Kingsmen, I'd be surprised to have any issue with you blabbing."

At the words, Flick shut the door and Anca watched as the pearly armor faded to dull steel. Her assumptions about their ages were correct; the inquisitor who spoke earlier was in his fifties, a beard adorning his face and silver hair. The other was much younger, hardly any older than she and Flick. The young one stretched, glanced at them, and smiled. "Thank you, Mr. and Mrs... I'm so sorry, remind me of your names?"

Flick glanced at Anca, one eyebrow raised, before he held a hand out. "Flick Alastar, and my wife, Anca."

"Ah, that's right! Forgive me, it's been a long day. I'm Inquisitor Martic, and this is Inquisitor Cole." Martic rubbed the back of his neck and then shook Flick's hand. "We are very grateful for the hospitality you're extending to us."

"The pleasure is ours," Flick replied.

***

They settled for an awkward dinner where Drop and Shatter stared at their plates. Flick cleared his throat. "We pray to HaMelech for our meals each night," he said. "I recognize that you aren't followers of HaMelech, but I do ask for your respect as we worship Him before eating."

Cole nodded slightly. "This is the nation of Dusnar. My expectation is that you respect our worship as well should we exercise it while in your home; we will do the same for you as well."

Flick gave a little nod in return and took Anca's hand. Drop and Shatter shared a glance with one another before they took hands, and, after a moment, Cole and Martic joined them. Anca couldn't help but give a bit of a smile as they all bowed their heads, and Flick murmured, "HaMelech, we praise you for your provisions today and always. Thank you for your protection, your faithfulness, and the blessings you've bestowed on us. Bless this food to our bodies, and allow us to rest in your safety from now until your embrace. Amen."

Neither inquisitor repeated the closing, and they kept their heads bowed for a few moments more. Then the group settled into eating. The children didn't speak much, though Flick did ask the inquisitors, "What exactly are you searching for your quarry for?"

"High treason," Cole said. He sipped at his cider. "Apparently, this Flick character denounced Solaris in the presence of the High Council in Zanther. High Inquisitor Alastar was rather tight-lipped about it while speaking to the Blackrock Council." With a little shrug, he began to eat. "I suppose it's a matter of pride, but, who knows; the High Inquisitors tend to be fickle."

Anca glanced at Flick, a sad smile on her lips. Flick's grip on his cider tightened and he cleared his throat. "I suppose they must be. Regardless, how long do you two suppose you'll be in Apple Ridge?"

"At least a week," Martic said. "Cole wants to leave sooner, but we were ordered to spend a week in each town. Though... I have to admit, I'm surprised by how large Apple Ridge is. Wasn't it supposed to be a pretty small town, Cole?"

"Mhm, smaller than this." The older of the inquisitors nodded to himself. "I was here many years ago, and they had only just put up the wall around the fort. I can't believe they're building a larger wall."

He was right; when Anca and Flick had arrived all those years ago, they hadn't needed to make a large wall. Then, as time passed, the wildlife became bolder and more travelers meant that the town had to create a better barrier. Anca looked at Flick. "It's certainly changed since more people come to Apple Ridge."

"It really has."

"Not as big as Zanther," Martic commented. "It's pretty, all the same."

***

After dinner, Anca settled in the sitting area with Drop, Shatter, and Flick. Her husband quietly cleaned his weapon, listening as she read from the Holy Texts. While Anca was nervous about the inquisitors joining them, Flick reassured her that normalcy was important. Besides, it was obedience to HaMelech, not to fear, when they read together.

As Anca flipped to the passage they had left off the night before, she caught sight of something in the corner of her eye. Cole was leaning against the doorframe, listening quietly to Drop and Shatter speaking. Martic had retired early, stating he was exhausted from the work they'd done during the day.

Flick glanced toward Cole and nodded slightly before he turned his attention to Anca. Quietly, Anca began to read about the spies HaMelech had sent into a city, and the woman who protected them from the citizens. As she read, she was ever aware of Cole's lingering eyes as though he was focusing intently on what she was saying. Then, as the small family prayed before bed, Cole slipped away.

***

Each day was the same; the inquisitors would join them for breakfast, lunch, and then dinner. Anca worried that she would wake and find

Flick gone and, each day, she found that it wasn't the case. Martic and Cole would speak quietly about the lack of leads, the inability to find any possible individuals who knew of Flick, and, ultimately, the lack of reason to remain in Apple Ridge.

Anca found it incredibly odd, especially as Martic and Cole would seemingly forget Flick's name, or their last name, constantly. Whether it was HaMelech acting or their inability, again, she didn't know. Either way, Flick opened each meal with thanks for HaMelech's provision and, before they laid down to rest each night, he would ask that HaMelech's will be done regardless of what it meant for their family.

There was only one instance in which Anca had been startled by the inquisitors' actions, and it was after Flick had left for the morning and Shatter had gone with him. Drop was still at home with Anca, carefully getting her things together to attend a class at the Temple of HaMelech.

The inquisitors had yet to leave their room.

It was perhaps the best day Anca had healthwise in several months. She tested her legs, holding herself upright carefully with the table for support. Drop watched her, shifting. "Mother, are you sure you're alright?"

"Currently, yes," Anca said back. "I'll sit in a moment, I want to let my legs stretch. It's been a while."

She sucked in a breath and took one step. It was shaking, but it was perhaps the most she'd done in a while. Anca smiled faintly. "Praise HaMelech," she whispered. She lightly took Drop's hand and sank back into her chair, then she wheeled towards the door. "Leave the door open when you go, please. I'm surprised the inquisitors haven't left their room yet, especially when they are often up around the same time your father and I are."

Drop nodded and gave her a tight hug. "I will. Please, be careful."

"I won't be standing again until someone else is here," Anca reassured. "I know better than to test my strength."

They pulled away from one another and Anca watched Drop go before she wheeled out and into their garden. She was grateful for the ability to go outside safely, especially as she paused to pick a couple of carrots from the garden and knocked them on her leg. They'd do well for dinner, she supposed, as she continued to go through the meager path. When she turned around, both inquisitors were standing beside the gate. "Oh! Good morning, I didn't realize you were awake!"

"We have been," Martic replied, shifting as he tended to do even when in his armor. "I assume your husband left?"

"Yes, a little while ago," Anca said. She started wheeling to them, tilting her head. "Is everything alright? We didn't keep either of you awake during the night, did we?"

Martic shook his head, but Cole remained still. Finally, the older of the two spoke. "I briefly heard your conversation with your husband, about your difficulties in growing your family."

Anca paused, and she looked down for a moment. "Ah, I do apologize."

"As do I," Cole said gently. "I hope you know that you aren't the only family to undergo that period, whether Solari or not. My wife and I waited for five years before we welcomed our daughter into the world."

His words made Anca look up, and she offered a sad smile. Though she couldn't see his face through the shroud he wore, she was sure he was giving her the same look she often received. Still, despite the nature of the conversation, she nodded. "I do appreciate it. It's been a trying time, but HaMelech will see us through it. I'm glad to hear you were blessed with your own child after a period of mourning."

He nodded faintly towards her before clearing his throat. "I believe this will be our final day in Apple Ridge. We'll stay for breakfast tomorrow and then return to Blackrock."

"If that is your course of action," Anca said, "I'll be sure my husband remains home to see you off."

The two inquisitors turned to go just as Anca exhaled, realizing she had held her breath. Her vision hazed and she caught herself, barely, before she fell from her wheeled chair. Her sound of discomfort in the sudden lurch forward made the Solari men pause and turn, and suddenly she was helped back into her chair. As usual, her head swam and it was hard to entirely register what they were saying, but she briefly caught Martic asking if they should find a healer. Cole, she assumed, nodded, and Martic hurried away.

When her vision and hearing returned, she found that he had returned with Marin, whose worried face spoke far louder than words. "Anca, are you alright?"

"I... think so," Anca said. She swallowed, rubbed her forehead, and looked at the two inquisitors. "Thank you... I think I would have been fine."

"You were hanging from your chair," Cole said simply. "You would have landed in the mud and asphyxiated."

Anca didn't argue as Marin reached her and began to check her over. Then, after a moment, Marin said, "I think we should get you to the Temple and check your blood pressure, alright?"

"I suppose," Anca murmured, "though I don't know if we'll be able to do much."

Slowly, the two women started to the Temple of HaMelech; the inquisitors went the other direction.

As they left, Marin looked down at Anca from pushing her chair. "Anca, did I ever mention to you one of the spiritual gifts HaMelech gave me?"

"You never did," Anca said. "I know you have the prayer tongue, otherwise... no."

Marin smiled ever so slightly and leaned in to murmur in Anca's ear, "I can see ethereals, both dark and light." Anca looked at her, catching the bit of mischief in her friend's face before Marin stood upright.

"Why are you telling me this now?"

"Because I've been amazed that those inquisitors haven't arrested Flick," Marin answered. She shook her head, and Anca sighed in agreement.

It was strange, but she hadn't had much time to question it. Then, she looked at Marin and raised an eyebrow. Marin wouldn't mention this gift unless the story wasn't over, and so Anca waited for her friend to finish speaking.

Just as she'd hoped, Marin looked around and continued quietly. "I had been thinking about it, and I asked HaMelech to open my eyes while with the two. Funnily enough, HaMelech did allow me to see what was going on. Anytime they get a lead, the ethereal drowns it out with his trumpet. It's amazing, really."

They entered the Temple and Anca chuckled.

HaMelech certainly had a sense of humor, didn't he?

Slowly, the two went into a room and Marin checked Anca over. Blood pressure seemed to be normal, as did her iron levels, but Anca didn't put any stock into it. She laid there quietly for Marin to check over her before her friend paused. "Anca, did you realize that you're..."

"I'm what?"

Marin pointed towards Anca's seat, and the woman frowned before her eyes widened. After a hushed exchange, Marin handed Anca a slim parcel. Anca cleaned herself in the bathroom and slowly returned. She looked at Marin, beginning to chew on her lip. "I haven't had a course, a proper one, for over four years. I mean... there were some here and there but... Marin, what do I do?"

"What do you mean, 'what do I do'? Anca, do you know what this means?"

Anca shifted in her seat, and then her face fell. "It isn't safe to try, you said it yourself. If I conceive, I could die. There are any number of things that could happen if I manage to conceive, and... and..." she trailed off, looked down, and squeezed her eyes shut. "Every time we have, I've lost the pregnancy. Why would HaMelech allow me to carry again after so many years?"

"I don't know, Anca."

The two sat in silence for a moment, and finally Anca whispered, "I want desperately to believe that maybe, Flick and I could have a child. HaMelech wouldn't allow me to possibly carry without reason, right?"

"He's a good God, Anca, but His ways are so much higher than ours," Marin said back. She held Anca's hand and rubbed it with her thumb, then she hugged her tightly. Anca leaned into the touch, closed her eyes, and cried.

***

She informed Flick of what was happening the moment the children and the inquisitors slipped to bed, and he listened silently. Finally, as she dared lift her eyes to stare at him, he stroked her cheek. "What do you want to do?"

"I'm not sure," Anca breathed. "I'm terrified to think that this could be HaMelech telling me we can have a child, especially with my health. I don't want to get my hopes up and then lose them as I have so many times."

"Do you still want a child with me?"

Did she? It scared her, knowing that it could possibly happen. Drop and Shatter were older; would they feel unwanted if she and their father had a baby? What about her own health? Would HaMelech welcome her into His Embrace if she went into labor bringing a new life into the world? Of all the possibilities, what was the likelihood that something horrible happened, anyway? Even with those thoughts,

Anca could feel the desire to raise one more child with Flick, complete their family with a final baby, whispering.

It never faded, even when she tried to convince herself otherwise. Finally, she nodded, and Flick embraced her. "Then we will wait until Marin and the other doves say it's safe, alright? Let your courses return to normal and remain predictable, and from there we can try. It'll be alright, my love."

Anca leaned into his arms, pressed her face into his neck, and simply sat. Flick was praying over her again, prompting her to sigh as that supernatural peace washed over her once more.

It would be okay.

***

The next morning, Flick, Anca, Shatter, and Drop bid the two inquisitors goodbye. Martic spoke softly to Flick, giving him instructions on how to contact them should they need anything. It was Cole who approached Anca, his voice incredibly quiet. "Thank you for keeping us in your home, Mrs. Alastar. If it isn't any trouble... Could I ask you for a copy of the Holy Texts? For intellectual purposes, of course."

The request made Anca blink at him, her eyes wide. An inquisitor wanted a copy of Kingsmen text? She supposed she'd heard crazier, given who her husband was, but this wasn't something she expected. After she cleared her throat, she nodded. "Of course, we're happy to gift you one... for intellectual purposes."

She could have sworn that Cole was smiling as she asked Shatter to fetch a copy of the Holy Texts, but she said nothing until she gave him a carefully wrapped package. "May HaMelech protect the two of you on your travels," she said softly. "I pray that our paths may cross again under different circumstances."

"As do I. May the True God bless you and your husband in our desire to grow your family," Cole said in return, his voice just as quiet as before.

Anca watched the two go, finding Flick's hand and holding it lightly until their guests walked from sight. Then, she looked at her husband. "He asked for the Holy Texts."

"He did?" Flick asked, raising an eyebrow. He gave a little hum. "HaMelech works in strange ways. I'm glad you were obedient to Him when you felt prompted to offer them shelter."

"As am I," Anca murmured. She looked at Drop and Shatter, a small smile flickering over her face. "You two were so incredibly brave. I'm so proud of you, both of you."

Drop exhaled, her shoulders relaxing. "I can't believe they found us."

"HaMelech protected us," Flick said softly. "They might have discovered that we were here, but I have no doubt in my mind that they weren't actually aware of who I am." He chuckled. "Praise HaMelech."

Chapter Ten

Eight Years, Two Months

Anca smiled as Drop dipped her head to accept her first pin for the Knights of the Long Road. Beside her, wearing his new mantle as well, Shatter waited his turn. Flick's chest was puffed in pride, his uniform decorated with his pins as he handed Olare Drop's metal.

They had both decided to follow HaMelech as Knights of the Long Road. Just before the ceremony, too, Flick had bestowed them each their mantles, sealing their bloodright as full cotes. Now they were allowed to shift between forms like he could. He said it was about time, as it was, having thirteen and fourteen-year-olds.

While Anca wasn't a cote herself, she had worked tirelessly on the mantles for her stepchildren. Stitching feathers together by firelight had been tricky, but she was glad to do it, especially when they saw the final mantles.

As Anca watched them stand beside the other teens who decided to serve as knights, she couldn't help but wonder what exactly the next year would bring.

The three Alastars came down from the stage and Anca hugged them tightly. "I'm so proud of you!"

"Thanks, Mother," Drop said, tucking a strand of hair behind her ear. Shatter didn't speak, but his grin told Anca all she needed to know. "You're really certain that it's alright that I'm not serving as a dove?"

"I'm positive! I'm glad that you found your calling and desire to follow it," Anca said, cupping her cheek. Drop smiled at her and Anca looked up at Flick. "A family of knights, then, my love."

Flick grinned, kissed her forehead, and looked over their children. "A family of Knights, and a lovely dove. I cannot explain how pleased I am to have a family obedient to HaMelech."

The small family made their way home, where they ate dinner and discussed the day. Halfway through eating, though, Anca felt incredibly ill.

She did her best to swallow the nausea down, nodding politely at Shatter as he continued to discuss some of the training Olare was putting him through. Eventually, he paused. "Mother, are you alright?"

"I think so, my little raven," Anca said. She swallowed, grimaced, and then shook her head. "Just an upset stomach, is all."

Flick frowned. "Do you need to lie down?"

"Perhaps," Anca murmured. Drop and Shatter glanced at one another, and then looked at Flick. He shook his head and stood.

"Let me help you into bed then, my love."

The two made their way to the bedroom, where Flick lifted her from the wheeled chair and laid her down. He sat beside her on the bed, stroking her hair, and frowned. "You're just feeling ill? Nothing else, no headaches, no lightheadedness?"

Anca nodded and sighed, grimaced, and then looked at him. "I'm sure it's just the nerves calming down now that the excitement is over," she said quietly. She took his hand as he stroked her hair again, squeezed it, and closed her eyes. "I'll be alright after I rest, I'm sure."

Flick kissed her head, pulled the blankets over her, and then made his way to the door. Then, after a moment, he paused and looked at her. "Anca, when was your last course?"

His question made Anca freeze, and she slowly looked back at him. When was her last course? Thinking about it, fear began to bubble through her. Finally, she whispered, "It's been at least a month, Flick."

His face flashed from concern to excitement before it returned to worry and he made his way back to Anca. Once more he sat beside her, this time taking her hand as he leaned close to her. "Do you think you might be pregnant?"

"Maybe? I don't know. I hadn't thought of that being a possibility," Anca admitted softly. "I was so focused on making sure the mantles were done, and I've been busy at work. I didn't pay any attention to my last one, and, honestly, I could have missed the previous month, too. I don't know."

How foolish! They'd returned, she should have been keeping better track of them! She ran a hand through her hair and then caught herself, doing her best to keep from vomiting, before she mumbled, "I'm sorry, my love."

"Please don't be sorry," Flick said. He chuckled, kissed her head, and shook his own. "If we are expecting a child, then we are expecting a child. I can fetch some barley for you to use, if you'd like—"

"Marin said the doves made a form of test to check for pregnancy," she interrupted. "I suppose it's more accurate than the barley itself. Blackrock shipped some over, and they've yet to use any. We could ask her for that, instead."

"Do you want Marin to know?"

Anca bit her lip.

As much as she wanted her dearest friend to be involved, she didn't want to burden Marin with mourning if this pregnancy was lost as well. Finally, she sighed. "No, we should ask someone else."

He nodded again at her before he laid down and pulled her close. As she lay there, listening to his heartbeat, all Anca could do was give a quiet prayer that things would be alright. Flick was praying too, as she could feel his chest moving rhythmically like he was speaking. She closed her eyes, sighed, and did what she could to relax.

***

The next morning, Anca awoke to Flick speaking to Drop and Shatter outside of the bedroom door.

"It's a possibility," he said gently. "We don't know for sure."

Shatter responded first, his voice just as soft. "Will she be okay if she is? I mean... as much as I want a little brother or sister, I don't want to lose Mother."

"She should be," Flick answered.

"And if she isn't?" Drop asked. "I remember what it was like, just the three of us. I don't want that, not again. You were a good father when it was just you but... I want Mother."

Anca wiped at the tears streaking down her face. "HaMelech, please, don't let this be my end," she whispered. "Keep me safe with this potential blessing, keep this potential child safe as well."

"She'll be fine," Flick reassured. She could hear them moving, and she assumed they were embracing. "HaMelech has a plan, and His will is perfect. We shouldn't fear the future, just know that He is in control. We can cover her in our prayers, and if there is a baby, we will cover the child in prayers as well. Either way, I need you both to remain silent about this, please. We've experienced many losses, and until we know that HaMelech has blessed us with another family member, I don't want others to know. Alright?"

Not waiting to hear their answers, Anca carefully put her shawl over her nightgown and slowly wheeled out. Drop and Shatter turned to face her and she opened her arms for them. They flung themselves into her hug, and she held them tightly as she closed her eyes. "It'll be alright, my little fledglings," she murmured. "HaMelech is holding me regardless of what happens, alright?"

"Okay," Drop whispered. "Just... I don't want to lose you. I like having you as our mother."

"I love being your mother, dearest," Anca whispered back. "It'll be alright."

Shatter held a little tighter. "Promise?"

"I promise as much as my physical body can, pet," she breathed.

As she pulled away from them, stroking their hair from their face and brushing tears from their eyes, Anca looked at Flick. He had a small parcel in his hand as he shifted, and then he held it to her. "This is the test. You'll take it into the bathroom."

"Like the barley?"

"Like the barley... but she said you'll know within a handful of minutes if it's a yes or a no. She said there's something that will change color if you are." Flick offered her a smile, but Anca could see that he was nervous, too. His hand shook as she took the test, and she pressed his hand before she inhaled. "Do you want me with you?"

Slowly, Anca nodded. She didn't want to be alone if it was another 'no', and if it was a 'yes', she wasn't entirely sure that she'd be able to remain conscious enough to call for her husband. Besides, as far as she could remember him telling her, he never felt the thrill of seeing whether or not his partner was pregnant. Both Drop and Shatter's mothers suddenly informed him of the pregnancy, or the subsequent child. This was a first for both of them.

She wheeled into the bathroom and Flick followed. Drop and Shatter milled about in the other room, where Anca could hear them pacing quietly. She used the test and set it down beside the washbasin, and then she looked at Flick. "What if I am expecting?"

"Then we will have another member of the family," Flick said softly. "HaMelech is in charge, and I trust Him."

"My body may not be able to handle carrying a child. If I'm not getting enough blood to my brain, what happens when I have a child I'm carrying?"

"We'll find a way, Anca. HaMelech has a plan, and if you're pregnant, I trust His plan to be good." Flick crouched before her and stroked her cheek. "I love you, Anca Alastar. If something happens, and we need to make changes, then we will. But now I just want to wait with you. Will you be pleased if you're with child?"

Anca nodded a little bit, offering a shaky smile to her husband. "I've wanted a child with you since we were wed. I suppose I'd given up entirely on the potential. I never brought up adoption as financially..."

"Financially we would be struggling if we were to adopt up until now," Flick finished. He nodded slightly. "HaMelech has timing that we will never understand... and speaking of timing... Do you want me to look first?"

She spared a glance at where the test was lying, the knot in her stomach beginning to grow. Despite her fears, she whispered, "Please."

Flick lifted the test, inhaled, and looked at it. Then, silently, he turned it to face Anca.

There was a little pink line.

For a moment, Anca simply stared. Then, tears began to prick her eyes, and she began to cry. They were ugly, hot tears that stung her cheeks and made her feel silly, but Flick pulled her tightly into his arms and clung to her. The warmth of his touch made her feel like maybe, just maybe, everything would be alright. From outside, Drop and Shatter knocked on the door. "Is everything alright?"

"Give us a moment, children," Flick replied, rubbing Anca's back. He held her a little tighter and Anca simply basked in the revelation.

She was pregnant. There was life growing in her; life that, possibly, would make it to birth. There was fear there, too, but more excitement than she realized. After a brief moment, Anca looked at the test again and then at Flick. "I'm carrying a child. Flick... I'm carrying your child."

"Praise HaMelech for His blessings," Flick whispered back. He cupped her cheeks in both hands, giving her a tender kiss. Anca returned it and stared at the test once more, swallowing past a lump in her throat.

Then, she looked at him. "We should tell them."

Flick kissed her once more before he opened the door. The first thing Anca could see were her children's worried eyes, as they peeked around the doorframe. It broke her heart to see them so concerned, but as she smiled, the worries melted off of their faces. "I'm carrying your brother or sister."

Both Drop and Shatter hurried in to hug her, prompting her to hold them each as she wrapped her arms around them. Their family was growing, and, if she had missed the month prior, she was two months into her pregnancy. She had been feeling fine up until recently, though, so she assumed that it was a rather new happening. Regardless, Anca kissed both Drop and Shatter's heads. "I love you, it'll be alright."

***

Their routines changed slightly, and Anca wasn't sure how she felt about it.

The visits to the Temple of HaMelech became more frequent, especially once the doves discovered her pregnancy. Many appointments were to ensure she received care enough to manage her fainting spells and that the baby within her womb was healthy. Each time, Anca waited with bated breath as Marin or one of the other midwives confirmed that she was still carrying her child.

Anca wasn't one to hide that it frightened her.

Each appointment, each prayer, each dizziness that hit her made her worry about what might come the next day, but she did her best to give it to HaMelech. He was her rock, after all, and she desperately needed to remember that.

Flick was still working, but he'd make it a point to check on her around noon each day. Then, when he came home, he would greet Anca affectionately and then spend a moment murmuring to their baby. Drop and Shatter were slightly more withdrawn, uncertain on how to interact with the growing child. From time to time, Drop would read out loud to Anca and Shatter would, in his own way, speak softly to the baby as well. Nights brought family prayer revolving around Anca and the baby.

***

She was five months pregnant when Marin put her tools down, a sad smile playing on her lips. "The baby's doing great, Anca."

"Why do you look disappointed then?" Anca asked softly. She shifted, sat up on the table, and exhaled to regain her vision. "What is it?"

"I think Blackrock can provide you better care than any one of us here can," Marin admitted, looking down. "As much as I want you to stay here, in Apple Ridge, I know that Blackrock is the safest place for the two of you to be as you wait to deliver."

The words made Anca blink, and she sighed.

Blackrock was a bigger city, and their doves were managing more advanced technology than here. That also brought the potential for

Flick's pay to increase, even with the added dangers of more Solari worshippers. Finally, Anca nodded. "I'll speak to Flick about it."

"Please know that I'm not trying to make you go," Marin said, her eyes wide as she looked at Anca. The smaller blonde couldn't help but smile as she took Marin's hand, holding it tightly as her friend murmured, "I want to see you and Flick hold this child. I want to see you experience motherhood in a new way after raising Drop and Shatter."

"I know," Anca murmured.

***

She waited for Flick to arrive for lunch, fiddling with her quill as she thought over her letter to Adriata. If she wanted her sister there during her birth, she needed to write now. Did she tell Adriata they would be moving to Blackrock? Flick hadn't agreed to doing that, but there really wasn't much of a conversation to be had; it was the next step, Anca knew, in their walk with HaMelech. When her husband came in, gave her a kiss, and then washed his hands, Anca sighed. "My love?"

"It's about going to Blackrock, isn't it?" Flick asked, not looking toward her.

Anca frowned to herself. She hated how he knew some things before she had brought it up. It was the Breath of HaMelech working again, though, otherwise Olare and Rolandus had brought it up.

Before she could ask, he glanced at her. "I've received orders to go. Rolandus and Olare brought me signed documents from Blackrock requesting my help what with an influx of Solari worshippers. They believe I am most suited for the task given our background." He gave a little smile and then sighed. "I figured that the letter came in response to something you needed confirmation for. Was I correct?"

Slowly, Anca nodded. "Marin and the others at the temple suggested that we go to Blackrock for the rest of my pregnancy."

Flick's eyes softened and he sat beside her. He took her hand, rested a hand on her stomach, and murmured, "If that is where HaMelech needs us to be, then that is where we need to be. We will speak to Drop and Shatter tonight, and I can head to Blackrock in the morning to find us a home."

"From what I was told, many homes have several floors," Anca said. "With my chair..."

"I'll find a way to get us a beautiful home that you can fully explore, I promise."

Drop and Shatter returned home that evening with Flick, and as Shatter took his boots off, he asked, "When do we leave?"

"What?" Anca asked, glancing at Flick.

Flick shook his head. "I didn't speak to either of them about moving."

Shatter looked between them. "Drop and I figured things were going to change, didn't we, Drop?" His sister nodded slightly and Shatter continued. "Are we going to Blackrock?"

Anca laughed a little and nodded. "I suppose we are. Are you both okay with that? If you aren't, I'm sure Marin—"

"We're coming with you," Drop said, shaking her head. "HaMelech called you and Papa, and we are going to go with you. He hasn't told us to stay."

Flick sighed. "What on torus did I do to end up with two wise children like you?" He hugged them tightly and looked at Anca. "I can go to Blackrock tomorrow, then. I'll send for you when we're ready."

"Marin, Olare, and Rolandus might join us to bring our belongings from here," Anca said.

It was a sudden change, but she felt at ease with it.

***

Flick sent for them after two weeks, and with the help of the town, and their friends in driving the oxen toads and wagons, Anca packed their belongings. Drop and Shatter sat quietly on the bench seat with her as she drove the cart, the two telling tales and asking Anca about the sights they may see.

"I heard they have wondrous technology in Blackrock," Drop said, pulling her mantle tighter over her shoulders. "One of my teachers said that they're using Ashuran kinetic crystals more than any other city in the nation. Do you think our home will have kinetic crystals, too?"

"Perhaps," Anca replied. There were some in Apple Ridge, but most of those were used in the Temple of HaMelech for the dove healers. Having crystaltech would be a very different happening, especially if they allowed for lights to remain on in the evening and better chances for their city to remain secure. "I think I'm most interested to see the copper and bronze they use in their vehicles. I heard once that all their wagons walk on legs like Aunt Adriata's did."

Drop and Shatter gave quiet sounds of fascination before Shatter asked, "Do you think we will still be able to serve there?"

That was a good question; Apple Ridge allowed for adolescents to serve. Whether Blackrock did, Anca wasn't sure.

She finally shook her head. "I don't know. I wish I had an answer for you. Perhaps, as you have been given a Knights of the Long Road pin, you will be able to serve as an exception." In the back of her mind, Anca wondered if she'd be allowed to serve, too. If they had enough people doing administrative work, she may be out of a job for a little while herself.

"How are you holding up? Olare called as his ram passed the wagon.

"Doing fine, simply trying to decide what Blackrock may be like," Anca replied.

Her friend nodded faintly. "It'll be unlike anything you imagined, but wondrous all at the same time. HaMelech has blessed it as a city of sanctuary, though you will find more Solari worshippers here than any other in Dusnar. There are Telfarians, too, in a separate district. They keep to themselves, mostly, but they're still there." He gave a mischievous grin. "Perhaps one day, the two of you will be asked to patrol that section of the city. The guard tends to be made up of all three factions, while other groups have only Kingsmen or Solari. It's a unique place."

Drop and Shatter were enamored by his words, and they continued to ask Olare, and then Rolandus, questions during their travel.

***

It was a long, winding road through a caldera when they reached Blackrock. The city itself was set in the bowl formed by a long-forgotten volcano, surrounding a sulfuric lake. Anca looked out over the city as they drove through it, stopping finally at the edge of the Kingsmen district where a large house of black wood stood.

Everything was dark here. The wood, the rocks; there was hardly a more fitting name for a city of this color.

As Anca and their small party pulled up to a home, Flick came out to meet them. He was wearing his mantle, his inky black feathers covering him entirely as his dark eyes peered over his beak. Anca tilted her head slightly, raising an eyebrow, and he shook his head. "The rakow here have decided I'm an excellent mugging target if I'm not in my mantle."

"Rakow?"

Flick pointed at a bushy, striped tail that slipped over a fence. "They're an enjoyable lot; I think I miss the pickpockets in Apple Ridge over them, though." Then, he smiled, helped them all from the cart, and led them in.

A grand staircase was the first thing that caught Anca's eye, not so steep that she was frightened about falling. "We'll need to put a chair onto it; there is a group here who make crystaltech chairs that can go up stairs," Flick said. “I've already spoken to them, but we will need to save for that one. Let me give you a tour..."

Anca followed him around the house — Drop and Shatter wandered off to explore as their friends began to pull furniture from the carts — before Flick brought her up the stairs.

"The third floor has a guest study... but there are rooms for Drop and Shatter, and us, and..." He trailed off as he opened a door, revealing a small room with a window seat. "I figured you would be happiest nursing our baby here, especially with the view."

"Can we really afford this?" Anca asked, looking at Flick. "It's beautiful, but..."

"The Blackrock government decided that we would be paying for this home using a part of my weekly pay," Flick said. "So long as I am working, this home is ours. Once we have paid it off, we will keep it."

Anca smiled slightly and leaned into him. "Alright... it'll be okay."

Chapter Eleven

Blessings (Nearly Nine Years)

Time moved quickly once the Alastars were settled in Blackrock.

Drop and Shatter were allowed to join the Knights of the Long Road, just as they had in Apple Ridge, though Drop took on more responsibilities at fifteen. Flick often patrolled in his mantle, given the wanted posters that adorned the Solari district. Given his status as a 'traitor', the government simply knew him as 'Captain A'. Anca found work in the Grand Temple of HaMelech, working in the offices and checking in patients. She worked for as long as she could before she was too uncomfortable to do much more than lie down to rest.

The healers at the Temple were very kind in accepting her as a patient, too. Once they understood the nature of Anca's fainting spells, they ran several other tests to find that her blood pressure fluctuated far too quickly for her body to handle. There wasn't much treatment that they could do, but they did encourage her to maintain a healthy lifestyle as she had been despite her condition.

When Anca became seven months pregnant, she reached out to Adriata a second time to invite her to visit. She was very clear that the stay would be during her birth, but she desperately wanted her sister there if at all possible. The return letter never came, and instead Adriata arrived with Jean several weeks later. Anca also wrote to Marin, asking her friend if she would be willing to attend to her. Then, it was all a matter of anxiously waiting for the child to come.

Anca found that Jean had grown several inches since the last time they saw her, startling her out of the memories of Jean as a very young child to a girl of eight years. Drop and Shatter were thrilled to see their cousin and spent time taking her to the stables or pointing out the rakow that pilfered the garbage cans.

When Marin came, Olare and Rolandus joined her. The three took to sleeping downstairs in the sitting room, Marin taking the adjoining study for privacy, while Adriata and Jean remained on the third floor. It was a chaotically busy time, but Anca found that she adored it.

***

One night, while they were finishing dinner, a knock sounded on the door.

Anca looked at Flick, who raised a hand and stood. "I'll see who it is. Please, continue eating. I'll be back shortly."

The group exchanged glances but didn't argue as Flick stepped away, silent until the door opened and then shut. Who on torus would be at the door around dinner time?

"They've asked for me to join a patrol this evening," Flick said as he returned to the dining room table. He held a neatly folded parchment in his hands, his eyebrows raised as he read it a second time. "It appears one of the young women scheduled to serve tonight is feeling poorly, and they would like me to fill in for her."

"Are you certain?" Anca asked. "We were planning on playing some games after we ate." She settled back and put her hands on her stomach. "It won't be as fun as when you join us."

"We won't have anyone to try miming a rakow tonight if you go, Papa," Shatter teased, earning a chorus of laughter.

Flick good-humoredly pushed his shoulder and then shook his head. "I'm afraid not, my love. I'll finish eating and then be on my way. I've got the house key with me, so you're welcome to lock the door after I go."

Anca nodded at his words and gave him a kiss before he settled down again. Their conversation was light and full of laughter, but the entire time, Anca felt that something was off. The night had something waiting, she could feel it in her bones, and she didn't like the idea of Flick leaving.

As she waited beside the door, holding Flick's mantle for him, she shifted. The gnawing feeling was growing worse, making her stomach twist and curl. "Do you really have to go?"

"I do, I'm sorry," Flick said. He kissed her forehead and pulled his mantle on. "Are you alright? You keep asking."

Anca nodded slowly. "Just a strange feeling is all."

Her husband smiled at her. "I'll be back before you know it. The shift is six hours; that'll put me home about midnight. I've been gone longer."

"True, but... I don't know, my love."

"If something happens, send Rolandus to find me. When he has his mantle on, he has far better eyesight than I could ever express; he'll find me much faster than anyone else will."

Flick kissed her again and Anca nodded, fixing his mantle.

He had a point. Rolandus and Olare were perhaps the best individuals to have if something went wrong, and Marin and Adriata could hold their own as well. Drop and Shatter were there, they'd keep Jean out of trouble. Even with the reassurance, though, the feeling didn't leave even after Flick did.

As the group settled into games, Anca couldn't get comfortable. The gnawing feeling had progressed into cramps; they were unpleasant, but not at all consistent enough to be mistaken for labor. Still, Anca politely excused herself to make some tea and breathe in a quieter room.

Marin and Adriata joined her after a little while.

"Are you doing alright?" Marin asked.

"Cramping," Anca said quietly. "I didn't drink enough water today, and it was hot. I just need to take it easy is all."

"Are you certain?" Marin asked, raising an eyebrow. "Anca, my dear, you are forty-two weeks pregnant. The child should have been born already."

"These aren't labor pains and, if they are, this is the very beginning of labor," Anca countered.

Adriata glanced at Marin. "Should we get Flick, just in case?"

"No." Anca shifted in her chair to get comfortable again. "He needs to finish the shift."

Both Marin and Adriata shared a look, and Anca gave them a look back. "I think I know when to recognize that I'm in labor," she said. "The doves at the Grand Temple said I wouldn't be able to speak, even if under threat of punishment. I'm speaking now, aren't I?"

"It's different for everyone," Marin said.

***

The three remained in the kitchen, chatting, before Adriata slipped off to make sure Jean was in bed. The cramping had grown worse, but Anca didn't think anything of it. Instead, she asked Rolandus to get some hot water for her to bathe in and ease the pain, as that had worked for her before.

It was just after midnight when there was a knock on the door, and a courier handed Anca a letter. It was a hastily scrawled note from Flick, apologizing as he had run into some issues while on patrol and he was now stuck doing paperwork. Anca read the note, sighed, and shook her head with a smile.

It was just like the shift to end in that way; Flick was dedicated to his service, and she was incredibly grateful for him for that.

As she got herself ready to lay down, slowly transitioning from the wheeled chair to the bed, Anca was startled by a rather sudden gush of fluid. She stopped, blinked, and then hurried herself to the restroom.

Just as she was concerned, her water had broken

Anca made her way down the hall and stopped at the top of the stairs. "Marin? Marin, I need you, please."

Her friend was in her nightgown as she sleepily came from the parlor, rubbing her eyes. "Is everything alright?"

"... I apologize, I should have listened to you before." Anca shifted, winced, and exhaled. "Please, send Rolandus out to find Flick. He's in one of the offices..." Anca trailed off as a cramp, realizing now that it was a contraction, raced through her. "Quickly."

Marin frowned before her eyes widened. "Oh! Oh, goodness! Rolandus! Rolandus, wake up!" As she flew from Anca's sight, the blonde wheeled herself to the bedroom and then bathroom.

Water had been comforting, and so she waited for Marin to rejoin her, asked for hot water, and waited amid her contractions. The noise woke Adriata, who hurried down the stairs to check on her. As soon as she, too, realized what was going on, Adriata took Anca's hand and sat with her as Anca labored in the bathtub.

"Where's Flick?" Anca questioned, lifting her head to look at her sister. "Has he arrived?"

"Not yet," Adriata replied. She rubbed Anca's back as Marin returned with some fresh towels. "Rolandus is still looking for him. Oh, and Olare has Drop and Shatter downstairs; the running woke them."

Anca nodded, gave them a relieved smile, and then winced again. This was going as smoothly as labor could, she supposed. It hurt, there was pain, but the water was helping. Adriata poured some of the warm water over her back, letting her sigh and relax as contraction after contraction hit her. "Marin... what if Flick isn't here in time?"

"HaMelech help him, he'd better be," Marin replied. She offered Anca a bit of a smile. "I'm thinking the feeling you had earlier was your intuition knowing that tonight was the night." She checked Anca over and then stroked some hair from her face. "You're doing great, Anca. It won't be long before you're ready to push."

"May I stay in the water, please?"

"Is it helping the pain?"

Anca nodded as a contraction hit her again, sighed, and looked at the two other women. "More than anything else. I can tolerate the contractions with it."

"Then please, stay in the water!" Marin laughed.

A little smile flickered over Anca's face as they began to idly chat. She'd pause amid the contractions and return to talking afterwards, pausing only when an urge to push hit her. Then, she looked at Marin. "Has Flick gotten back?"

"No, I haven't heard them," Marin said. She shifted, pressing Anca's hips lightly as Anca grimaced again. "Are you alright?"

"I need to push, and I'd like my husband here." Anca gripped Adriata's hand as a commotion downstairs startled her, and she began to laugh.

Flick crashed into the bathroom, his eyes wide and face pale. "Anca, are you alright?"

"You're just in time!" Marin replied, laughing alongside the laboring woman.

Anca sighed and looked at Flick. "Your timing is impeccable. Can you get in here and hold me?"

"Are you sure?" Flick asked, looking at Adriata and Marin. "I don't want to make them uncomfortable—"

"Flick Alastar, kindly get into this tub and hold me as I push this baby into the world!" Anca snapped, grimacing as she allowed her body to bring the child closer to birth.

Flick's eyes widened. Then he stripped down to his undergarments, got into the water, and held her. She leaned into his chest, breathing hard as Marin stroked hair from her face and Adriata held her hand.

"You're doing great, Anca," the dove healer said, smiling. "You're crowning. Just take this slowly; your body is doing exactly what it needs to do."

Anca nodded as Flick rubbed her belly, his eyes growing wide as she contracted again. Then, he kissed her and murmured, "You're doing great. You can do this. Just keep breathing... How's your vision?"

"I don't want to open my eyes and find out," Anca whispered breathlessly. "I just want to labor without worrying that I'm going to fall unconscious."

Flick kissed her again, held her a little tighter, and murmured, "I've got you, if you do."

"Flick, you're going to want to move slightly so Anca can catch the baby," Marin said gently. "She's nearly done it."

Anca groaned as Flick shifted her before she reached down. In a final contraction, she caught the child and lifted it to her chest, panting and laughing. Her mirth was joined by the soft sounds of a baby, though they weren't wails. Anca slowly craned her neck to look at the wet infant on her chest, finding two little blue eyes staring at her. "Hello," she whispered. "Look at you... Flick, look at our child..."

"Your son," Marin said gently, laying a towel over the baby.

Anca instinctively rubbed the child with the towel as Marin helped her get comfortable, her eyes focused on the baby.

He was beautiful.

Flick looked over her shoulder, his voice incredibly soft as he whispered, "Anca, you did it. He's perfect."

She nodded slightly, tears beginning to streak down her face. "He really is."

"Once you deliver the afterbirth," Marin murmured, "I want to move the three of you to the bed. Flick, you're going to need to help Anca stand and get there. We'll tidy you up, tuck you in. Once you're settled, you're welcome to let Drop and Shatter meet their little brother."

Anca smiled faintly before she looked at Adriata. Her older sister had turned away, one hand over her mouth and the other on her hip.

"I've never seen childbirth, and it only solidifies that I'm glad to be rid of the ability to deliver myself," Adriata mumbled. "You did well, though, and I'm proud of you. I... believe I need to step out for a few minutes. Please let me know if you need any help getting up. Until then... I... excuse me."

She hurried out of the room, making Anca laugh to herself, before her gaze returned to the infant on her chest. He was looking around now, still silent despite having just entered the world.

"Perhaps the most judgmental child I've witnessed," Anca murmured. Flick shifted her slightly as she brought the babe to her breast to nurse, stroking his wet hair and breathing in his scent. He was absolutely perfect, and she was so incredibly in love.

They remained in the warm water until Marin cut the umbilical cord, at which point Flick carefully helped Anca stand and make it to their bed. Marin had prepared it earlier, readying it for the birth itself and for Anca to relax afterwards. Flick helped Anca settle before he changed out of his wet clothes and into his nightwear, settling beside her shirtless as he stroked her hair and rested his hand on the baby.

Anca knew he was enamored, even if he was silent. The way he continued to stare at the child and her spoke volumes, and she finally broke the quiet air. "We need to name him."

"We do," Flick whispered. "Did you have names you were considering? I know we discussed some but... none of them seem to be fitting."

Anca shook her head and then paused. "We had discussed the name Caxton, before, but as a middle name. I don't know if you like it enough—"

"No, I love the name Caxton," Flick interrupted softly. He traced the baby's little ear, making him move, and smiled a bit. "We can name him Caxton."

They sat together, silently, until Caxton finished nursing. Then, Anca quietly burped him and handed him to Flick. She watched as her husband cradled him gingerly, his eyes growing glassy with tears, and then he kissed his head. "Caxton Alastar. He's the perfect addition to our family."

Anca nodded, stroked Caxton's little foot, and laid back. Once Flick was done holding the child, Anca swaddled him carefully.

"Do you want to bring Drop and Shatter in first?" She asked. "They were perhaps the most anxious when I went into labor."

Flick moved to get up and Marin, who had been quietly cleaning the bathroom, interrupted, "I'll get them. I want the two of you to continue bonding with him while I do. This is time for your family to be a unit."

A grateful smile flickered over Anca's face and she settled back, holding the baby again as she leaned into Flick's side. He kissed her forehead, continuing to watch their precious child, before Drop and Shatter crept in. They sat on the bedside and then crawled into the bed beside Anca and Flick. There, Drop stared down at Caxton, her mouth parted slightly. Shatter leaned over Flick to get a better look, one eyebrow raised, before he looked at his parents. "He's going to be blond, isn't he?"

"I think he may," Flick said.

Drop nodded faintly. "He's got Mother's blue eyes." She looked at Anca. "I think he looks lovely."

"I do too," Anca murmured back. She watched Shatter quietly rest a hand on Caxton's back, his head tilted slightly. Then, after a moment, she asked, "What do you think, Shatter?"

"I think I'm suddenly a big brother, even though I knew it was going to happen," Shatter said. He chuckled and shook his head. "It didn't feel real before. I mean... we knew you were pregnant but... he's so small. I've got the feeling that we're going to have to keep a constant eye on him. You aren't going to spoil him, right?"

Flick chuckled and shook his head. "Of course not. He'll have the same harsh upbringing we gave the two of you." He rolled his eyes and tousled Shatter's hair. "I hope you both know that this doesn't change our family and who you are to us."

Drop looked at them, an easy smile on her lips. "We know. It's going to be different since he's here, but that'll change again. He's got to be taken care of; he's not exactly independent."

Anca nodded to them and kissed their foreheads. "Well, as that's out of the way, would either of you like to hold Caxton?"

"May we?" Drop asked, her eyes growing wide. "He's little, as Shatter said. I won't hurt him, right?"

"No, HaMelech made babies rather resilient, I've found," Anca said. She moved slightly for Drop to get comfortable beside her and then placed Caxton into her arms. A smile flooded her face as Drop stiffened and then relaxed as she held her baby brother, her face growing soft. "You're a natural, my love. You and Shatter both."

"I'm so afraid I may drop him," the teenager whispered. "I don't want to wake him."

Caxton had slipped to sleep as Anca held him, still resting as Drop held him carefully. "We'll soothe him to sleep if he does wake up," she reassured softly. "With what your father said, I hope you know that it isn't your responsibility to raise him. You're welcome to help however you wish, but ultimately you are both still children and are not responsible for his upbringing."

Drop and Shatter nodded silently, and Anca carefully passed Caxton to Shatter. The teen boy blinked at his brother, grinning, and looked up at Flick. "This should be a fun adventure."

"I would dare say it will be," Flick replied, chuckling. "I'm ready to teach you both to change diapers."

The family shared a soft laugh together before Flick and Anca rested with their children. Eventually, both Drop and Shatter yawned.

"Off to bed, both of you. You're excused from duties tomorrow due to this rather momentous night... Marin, would you be alright letting Olare and Rolandus up here? Adriata went to bed, didn't she, Anca?" Flick said.

Anca nodded faintly. "She was incredibly disturbed by watching, poor thing."

Marin slipped out and returned with the two men, and they sat beside the bed. Olare spoke. "He looks like a spitting image of you, Anca. Apologies, Alastar; I suppose your final child won't look at all like the Alastar bloodline."

Flick shook his head. "I'd much rather him look like his mother than any other Alastar," he replied. "He'll stay out of trouble, that way."

Anca passed Caxton to Rolandus, and Marin leaned in over his shoulder to study the boy again. Rolandus' eyes softened as he looked at Marin, his voice growing soft. "Perhaps one day, Marin."

"Once HaMelech releases us from our vows," she murmured back, a sad smile on her face. Anca's face grew tender as she watched the two, their shared moment a quiet testimony to their past, and she gave Marin a sad smile. Her friend returned it, then watched Rolandus hold the baby. After a moment, Rolandus passed Caxton to Marin before Olare finally took the boy.

The older man nodded faintly, cradling Caxton gently. Then, he looked at Anca and Flick. "Congratulations, you too. You should be very proud."

"Very grateful," Anca corrected softly. "It was only by HaMelech's blessing that he joined our family."

They remained together before the others retired, and Anca and Flick settled for the first night with a newborn. Anca woke several times through the night, settling back down beside Flick, who would pull her close, kiss her, and soothe her back to sleep.

Adriata and Jean met Caxton the next morning, and Anca patiently showed Jean how to hold her younger cousin. "You support his neck like this... there you go, good girl."

Jean smiled up at her and then looked down at Caxton. "Did Drop and Shatter see him?"

"Last night," Anca murmured. She stroked Jean's hair down. "They're still sleeping."

"Well... I'm glad that your prayers were answered," Adriata said from where she sat. She crossed one leg over the other, a little smile flickering over her face. "May this boy grow strong."

Their home emptied several days after Caxton's arrival, but not before the family group stood at the Temple of HaMelech to dedicate Caxton to HaMelech.

Anca smiled up at Flick, holding Caxton in her arms as he slept soundly. Flick kept her near his side, smiling fondly back at her as he wore his mantle and uniform. Drop and Shatter stood at attention in their own uniforms, while Rolandus, Olare, and Marin stood behind them as the silent godparents. Anca caught sight of Marin and Rolandus holding hands just before the priest spoke, and then she focused on the man speaking. Out of the corner of her eye, she could see Adriata and Jean standing in the back of the gathered assembly, uncomfortable but willing to witness.

"Today, we dedicate Caxton Alastar and his upbringing to HaMelech, the King of Kings. Before we do so, we desire to bring our prayers of thanksgiving to our gracious Lord for the birth of this boy, and the blessings that have been outpoured over them."

As Anca lowered her head, staring at her son, she sighed. "Thank you, HaMelech... for answering a mother's prayer."

About the author

Ellie Lerum is a fantasy author and blogger whose stories blend redemptive hope, emotional depth, and a touch of whimsy. A devout Christian and mother of dragons (well, griffins... and two spirited little girls), she writes tales that wrestle with grief, healing, and courage through richly imagined worlds. Ellie draws inspiration from her faith, real-life loss, and the works of J.R.R. Tolkien to craft narratives that are both adventurous and deeply human. Whether writing or exploring Idaho with her family, she finds the greatest joy in connecting with readers who see themselves in the stories she tells.

Follow her on Facebook and Instagram @AuthorEllieLerum, or at authorellielerum.com

Also by Ellie Lerum

The Cassy Series

Book 1: Phantom in the Dark

Book 2: Souls in the Ice

Book 3: Specter in the Shadows

Book 4: Wraith in the Light

Tales of Illeross

Turning Point

Gracefully Broken

A Mother's Prayer

Children Books

Animals of Illeross: An A-Z Alphabet

www.ingramcontent.com/pod-product-compliance
Lightning Source LLC
LaVergne TN
LVHW010946110826
845149LV00015B/3230